THE PET FINDERS CLUB

THE PET FINDERS CLUB

THE PET FINDERS CLUB

Looking for Lola!

BEN M. BAGLIO

Hodder
Children's
Books

A division of Hachette Children's Books

Special thanks to Liss Norton

Text copyright © 2005 Working Partners Ltd
Illustration copyright © 2007 Cecilia Johansson

First published in the USA in 2005 by Scholastic Inc

First published in Great Britain in 2007
by Hodder Children's Books

The rights of Ben M Baglio and Cecilia Johansson to be
identified as the Author and Illustrator of the Work respectively
have been asserted by them in accordance with the Copyright,
Designs and Patents Act 1988

1

ISBN-10: 0 340 93132 9
ISBN-13: 978 0 340 93132 5

Typeset in Weiss by Avon DataSet Ltd,
Bidford on Avon, Warwickshire

Printed in the UK by CPI Bookmarque, Croydon, CR0 4TD

The paper and board used in this paperback by Hodder Children's
Books are natural recyclable products made from wood grown in
sustainable forests. The manufacturing processes conform to the
environmental regulations of the country of origin.

Hodder Children's Books
a division of Hachette Children's Books
338 Euston Road
London NW1 3BH

Chapter One

"See you later, little Bud," Andi Talbot whispered, crouching down to stroke her Jack Russell terrier. "Be good for Mum." She truly hated leaving him every morning when she went to school, but at least he'd have her mum around all day today.

Andi and her mum, Judy Talbot, had moved from Texas in America to Aldcliffe, a suburb of Lancaster in England, just a few months ago. After using a local launderette for that time, Judy Talbot had decided it was time for a new washing machine. She'd taken the day off so it could be delivered that morning.

"I'd better get back, darling," Mrs Talbot said, "in case the machine arrives early."

"Just think – no more Saturday afternoons at Soak 'n' Suds!"

Her mum smiled. "Fantastic! A weekend will finally be a weekend!"

Andi kissed her mum. "See you later." She gave Buddy another pat, then ran across the playground to join Larissa, Kelly and Howard, friends from her class.

"Hi!" she shouted.

Howard jumped.

"Whoa, Howard," Andi said, surprised that she had startled him.

"Oh, hi, Andi," he said. "Sorry. Larissa's been telling us about the ghost her cousin's friend saw in Tangletree House last night." He ran his fingers through his hair, making it stick out at all angles. "I suppose I got a bit spooked."

"Andi doesn't look anything like a ghost," Kelly pointed out, switching her cat-print tote bag to her other shoulder. "You need glasses, Howard."

"Who says they saw this ghost?" Andi asked. She didn't believe in stuff like that, but it sounded like a good story. "Larissa's friend's cousin?"

"No, my cousin's friend," Larissa corrected her, as though it were obvious. "He said he saw a pair of huge glowing eyes staring out at him from a window last night."

Andi laughed. It sounded like something Larissa's cousin's friend had seen in a horror film.

Kelly squealed. "I bet it's Agnes Delaney!" she said excitedly. "She was murdered in Tangletree House a hundred years ago, or something."

It still sounded fake, but Andi felt the hairs on the back of her neck prickle. "How do you know?"

"It was in the local paper a few weeks ago. They ran a story about the house because it's going to be renovated for flats."

"I read that article, too," Larissa said. "Agnes's nephew murdered her for her money, apparently."

"I bet she's come back from the dead to drive the builders away," Howard said. "She probably doesn't want anyone messing about with her house."

"Yeah," Kelly agreed, her grey eyes wide. "I wouldn't want to work there. Too creepy!"

Chen, the last member of their science group, came running over, and dropped his camouflage rucksack on the ground. "Hey, are you talking about Tangletree House?" he asked. "Lonny Kennedy says she heard a ghost wailing in there when she passed by on her way to school this morning."

They all stared at him. A cold chill tingled down Andi's spine. She reminded herself again that she didn't believe in ghosts. But if other people had heard it . . .

"It must be true, then," Howard declared. "I'm gonna go and have a look round."

Chen laughed. "You wouldn't dare."

"Come with me if you want."

Kelly gave another shriek. "Don't go near there!"

Andi noticed her friend Natalie waving to her from across the playground. She ran to join her. "What's all the gossip about?" Natalie asked, flipping her shiny blonde hair over her shoulder. As usual, she looked as though she had just been to a salon, while Andi felt as though she looked like she'd done ten laps on a running track. "There's a ghost at Tangletree House," Andi explained.

Natalie made a face. "Whatever!"

"I thought that, too," Andi said. "But now Lonny supposedly heard it wailing."

Natalie laughed.

"No, listen!" Andi persisted. She told her about Agnes Delaney.

"Tell you what," Natalie suggested, picking a long blonde hair off her jacket and letting it blow away. "Let's walk past Tangletree House after school and see if we can meet this ghost. I bet we don't!"

"Uh, OK." Suddenly Andi hoped Natalie was right about there being no such things as ghosts.

"What are you two up to?" asked a voice, suddenly. A red-haired, freckle-faced boy was standing behind them.

"Tristan! I should have known it was you," Natalie said sharply, "creeping up on us like that."

"Me?" he said indignantly. "Creep?" He flung his arms out as though he'd just finished a song-and-dance number on stage. "Am I the sort of person who creeps? What are you looking so secretive about, anyway?"

"We're going ghost-hunting after school," Andi told him. "Want to come?"

Tristan's eyebrows shot up. "Ghost-hunting? I thought we hunted for lost animals."

Not long after Andi had moved to Aldcliffe, she'd helped Tristan and Natalie set up the

5

Pet Finders Club, to help people who'd lost their pets.

"Not today," Natalie said. "We're going to Tangletree House after school."

"We're not going inside," Andi added hurriedly, "just walking past."

"I can't," Tristan said. "Christine's having two pythons delivered." Tristan often helped out at the local pet shop, Paws for Thought. It was owned by his mum's cousin, Christine Wilson. "Do you want to come and see them?"

"No thanks!" Natalie told him, with a shudder.

Tristan laughed. "What, so snakes are worse than ghosts?"

"A zillion times worse!" Natalie insisted. "It's impossible not to believe in them, for a start!"

"Sit down quickly," called Mr Dixon as the kids filed into their classroom.

Andi and Natalie saw eyebrows rise across the room. Mr Dixon was usually much more cheerful than this, so Andi wondered if they were about to be told off for something. Miss Ashworthy and her class were also waiting for them in the classroom.

Tristan was sitting on the far side of the room, near the window.

"Fill up the empty chairs first," Miss Ashworthy told Mr Dixon's class. "The rest of you can sit on the floor."

Andi flashed a quick smile at Tristan, as she looked around for an empty chair. He grinned back.

"What's so funny, Tristan Saunders?" demanded Miss Ashworthy.

"Nothing!" Tristan said hurriedly, turning to face the front again.

The empty chairs were soon taken, so Natalie and Andi sat down on the floor. "This is going to ruin my skirt," Natalie complained.

Mr Dixon took the register and then addressed both classes. "Miss Ashworthy and I want to speak to all the Year Fives together." He still looked grim.

"Now," said Miss Ashworthy. "It seems as though the whole school is talking about Tangletree House this morning."

A murmur of excitement swept around the room, which Miss Ashworthy squashed with a glare down her long nose.

Mr Dixon looked round sternly. "Nobody is to

go to Tangletree House in the hope of proving the stories right or wrong. Building sites are dangerous places, as I'm sure you all know."

"Anyone who is seen on the site will find themselves in detention for a week," Miss Ashworthy warned. "So stay away."

Andi glanced at Natalie, who was fiddling with the beads on her skirt. Andi couldn't see her face, but she was willing to bet that Miss Ashworthy's threats wouldn't be enough to keep Nat away from Tangletree House that afternoon.

Natalie was waiting for Andi when she came out of the changing room after football that afternoon. "How did it go?" she called.

"Not bad. I scored two goals, so Mr Wallace will definitely put me in the game next week!" Andi gave her a high five. "How was Chess Club?"

Natalie groaned. "I was hopeless. I kept thinking about the ghost. Jordan Maloney beat me twice, and she's never going to let me forget it."

" 'Course she will. She's got a brain like a sieve. She forgets her homework or her PE kit at least once a week." Andi paused before asking the question she knew Nat was waiting for. "So, do you still want to go to Tangletree House?"

"You bet!"

"Where is it?" Andi asked.

"On Windrush Drive, on the other side of the park. We can pick up Jet and Buddy on the way."

Natalie lived closest to the school, so they fetched Jet, her black Labrador, first. He bounced around her while she tried to clip on his lead. "Calm down!" Natalie gasped. Jet dragged them along the pavement to Andi's house as if he were a sled dog.

"Hi, Mum!" Andi called as she opened the front door. "Did the washing machine come?"

"Yes, thank goodness," Mrs Talbot replied, coming into the hall with Buddy at her heels. "I've done three loads already. Oh, hi, Natalie." She patted Jet. "Are you going for a walk?"

"Yeah, to the park." Andi dropped her rucksack on the hall table and checked the phone to see if the message light was flashing. It could mean another case for the Pet Finders to solve. But there were no messages. *Uh oh*, thought Andi. *Now we'll really have to go and look at that house.* As she grabbed

Buddy's lead, she reminded herself for the tenth time that she didn't believe in ghosts.

The park looked beautiful in the early November sunshine. The trees were shades of orange, scarlet and gold, with some of the leaves falling gently to the ground. As soon as Andi let Buddy off the lead, he tore away from them, then circled around with his mouth open in a wide doggy grin.

"I wish I could let Jet off," said Natalie, "but I can't trust him to come back when I call."

Andi shivered, remembering the time Jet and Buddy had both got lost, and how she'd been convinced that she'd never see her dog again.

Buddy leapt up at her and Andi rubbed her fingers over his tan-and-white fur. "Thank goodness I got you back, boy."

As they climbed the hill towards the woods, Buddy began to bark at something behind them. Andi looked back to see what he'd spotted. A pint-sized dog was edging along a path on the far side of the pond. It was cream-coloured and looked just a little bit taller than Buddy, though it was hard to be sure from this distance. "What a cute dog!" Andi exclaimed. Instinctively she looked around for the dog's owner. "I wonder who it belongs to."

The dog didn't even glance at them, but disappeared into some shrubs. Immediately, Buddy bounded off after it. "No! Come back, Buddy," Andi called.

Obediently, he stopped, turned and trotted back, and Andi crouched down to hug him.

"He's so good," Natalie sighed. "Do you see that, Jet? Buddy knows how to behave when he's off his lead."

"I can't see anyone who could be that dog's owner," Andi said thoughtfully. "What if it's lost, and it turns out to be another case for the Pet Finders Club? Maybe we should go and catch it."

"We can't go chasing after every loose dog we see," Natalie pointed out. "If we did, there'd be some pretty angry owners around demanding to know why we were grabbing their pets."

"I suppose you're right."

"In any case, the dog's owner is probably behind those bushes," Natalie said as they went on. "And we're supposed to be ghost-hunting, not dog-hunting."

They were nearly into the woods when the little dog came rocketing past them. "That dog is definitely out without an owner!" Andi exclaimed. "I think it might really be lost." She held out her hand. "Here! Come on! Good dog."

Again, the dog took no notice. It shot in among the trees and disappeared. "Let's see if we can catch up with it," Andi suggested.

They started to run, but by the time they reached the trees, the dog had vanished.

"It's probably gone home," Natalie puffed, catching up with Andi and leaning against a trunk. "It was wearing a collar, so it must belong to someone."

"Perhaps," Andi said. But deep down, she knew she was just looking for an excuse not to go to Tangletree House. Larissa's story had scared her far more than she was going to let on!

The light was beginning to fade when they emerged on the other side of the woods and headed down Windrush Drive. Soon, they stood in front of a four-storey house with a pitched slate roof and windows like sinister beady eyes, silhouetted against the darkening sky. Andi gulped. It looked like something out of a film, even without all the stories about ghosts and murdered aunts.

"This is it," Natalie announced. "Tangletree House."

The house was surrounded by a tall wire fence with notices warning trespassers to keep out. From where they were, Andi could just make out a row of huge dark holes dug in the garden to the right of the house, bulldozers standing idle above them. Most of the garden had been cleared, but a tangle of overgrown shrubs and brambles still grew close to the house's north wall, separating the house from the building site. The whole area was deserted and the silence made it even more eerie.

"Let's get closer," Natalie suggested. There was a slight tremor in her voice and Andi glanced at her.

"You nervous?" she asked.

"No. I told you, there's no such thing as ghosts."

They started to walk towards the house. Suddenly, Buddy bounded forward, barking loudly and almost jerking the lead out of Andi's hands. "Stop it, Buddy," she scolded.

But Buddy kept on barking and then Jet threw back his head and howled.

"What's wrong with them?" Natalie whispered, turning pale.

"People say animals are sensitive to the supernatural," Andi stammered. "Maybe they can see something we can't."

Natalie's eyes grew wide with fear. "You don't mean . . . ?"

Andi nodded, her teeth chattering. "The stories about Agnes Delaney's ghost must be true!"

Chapter Two

The next day after school, Andi was doing her homework at the kitchen table when the phone rang. She jumped up to answer it.

"Hello, is this the Pet Finders Club?" asked a woman's voice.

Andi's heart flipped. "Yes," she replied, hoping she sounded calm and professional. "Can I help you?"

"Oh, I hope so. I've lost a pet."

"Is it a cream terrier cross?" Andi blurted out, remembering the dog she and Natalie had seen at the park the day before. They hadn't noticed it on their way home from Tangletree House last night – but they had both been running so fast, even Natalie would have made the school athletics team if the teacher who coached them had been watching.

The woman seemed surprised. "No, she's a cat. A pure-bred Russian Blue called Lola."

Andi picked up the pen from the message pad by the phone. "Can you give me your name and address, please?"

"I'm Helen Giacomo. And I live at 5 Scayne Place."

Andi scribbled it down. "How long has Lola been missing, Mrs Giacomo?"

"Two days. She must have escaped from my house somehow and I'm so worried. She's expecting kittens."

Andi's heart went out to her. Mrs Giacomo sounded very upset and Andi remembered only too clearly how awful she'd felt when she'd lost Buddy. "Don't worry," she said. "We'll find her for you. Can we come to your house to get some more information?"

"Absolutely. I'll be here for the rest of the day."

"I'll just call the other Pet Finders," Andi said, "and we'll come straight over. Give us half an hour." She put down the phone, her heart pounding with excitement at the thought of investigating another pet disappearance. Their last case had resulted in finding dozens of missing animals from Christine's pet shop. This case would be much easier, she thought hopefully. A pregnant cat wasn't likely to have strayed too far, and one single cat would be a lot easier to find than all those gerbils, snakes, and parrots had been.

Tristan was already waiting outside Mrs Giacomo's house when Andi arrived. He was holding a ring binder with a shiny red cover. "What do you think?" he asked, holding it up. "I got it from my mum and dad's estate agency office. I thought we could keep notes in it."

"Terrific! It looks really official."

Natalie soon came hurrying around the corner. "Sorry I'm late. I couldn't find my mobile."

Tristan raised his eyebrows in disbelief. "Do you mean it doesn't come with a built-in satellite location system?"

Natalie made a face at him. Tristan always gave her a hard time about the extravagant accessories she owned. "I found it in the end," she said. "It had

18

slipped down the side of my bed." She pulled it out of her pocket. "Don't forget this phone helped us solve our last case. If I hadn't been able to take a picture of that house, Fisher and Christine would never have known where we were."

"OK, OK." Tristan help up his hands. "You don't need to remind me." He and Andi had got into a lot of trouble for going into a run-down house where a thief had been hiding out.

A short, plump woman with grey hair answered the door when Natalie rang the bell at 5 Scayne Place. "We're the Pet Finders Club," Tristan introduced them.

"Come in. I'm so glad to see you." She led the way into her living room, where the walls were covered in shiny certificates and awards. A huge, rather gaudy gold trophy stood on the mantelpiece and there was a pretty silver-grey toy cat draped on the arm of the sofa. Andi stared at it, wondering if it looked like Lola. She stroked it idly, then jumped back, shocked, as it twitched its ears and began to purr: it was real!

"That's Lola's sister, Deena," Mrs Giacomo explained. "She misses Lola almost as much as I do."

The cat glanced up at Andi with mournful green eyes.

"Please sit down," Mrs Giacomo said.

"Do Lola and Deena look alike, Mrs Giacomo?" Andi asked, sitting beside Deena. Photos would be helpful for finding out what the missing cat looked like, but seeing an identical cat would be even better.

"Lola's fur is a bit paler and her ears are more pointed. She's smaller, too. Wait, I've got a photo here." Mrs Giacomo took a photo out of a drawer and handed it to Andi. Lola was looking straight into the camera. Her tail was curled over her front paws and her ears were pricked curiously.

"She's lovely!" Andi exclaimed.

"She is," agreed Mrs Giacomo. "And she's also very friendly."

"Like my cat, Lucy," Tristan whispered to Andi. "*She* was friendly too." Lucy had been missing for several months, since before Andi had moved to Aldcliffe.

Andi patted Tristan's arm. She knew he still missed Lucy badly, but there didn't seem much

chance of finding her now, after so long. She passed
the photo to Natalie.

"What a cute face!" Natalie exclaimed. She
handed it to Tristan.

"Can we keep the photo, please, Mrs Giacomo?"
Andi asked. "We'll need to scan it into my computer
when we make posters."

"Of course."

Tristan looked at the photo solemnly, then
tucked it inside the front cover of the red folder.

"You told Andi that Lola had escaped from the
house. Does that mean you don't usually let her
out?" Natalie asked.

"Only when I'm there to watch her. And then she
only goes into the back garden." Mrs Giacomo
smiled sadly. "She loves it out there."

"But she got out on her own this time?"
Tristan queried.

"She must have done. We had a couple of warm
days and I left the back door open with only the
screen door to keep the cats inside."

"Screen door?" Natalie asked. "What's that?"

"It's a door covered with fine mesh to keep
insects out," Andi explained. "We had one in Texas,

but I didn't realize anyone had them in England."

"My husband is American," Mrs Giacomo said, "and he had one specially made when we moved to this house."

"When did you first realize Lola was missing?" Natalie asked.

"It was quite early. I'm always up by six o'clock and I opened the door at about quarter to seven." Mrs Giacomo sighed. "I noticed she wasn't here at about seven thirty, but she could have been gone for a while."

Tristan wrote these details in the red book.

"The garden is fenced in," Mrs Giacomo continued. "But I suppose Lola could have climbed the fence if she'd got out of the house without me noticing."

"Could we have a look at the garden?" Andi asked.

"Of course."

They followed Mrs Giacomo out of the living room, across a narrow hall and into the kitchen. Mrs Giacomo opened the back door and led them into a grassy garden surrounded by a wood-panel fence about two metres high. "A cat could be over that in no time, with no one watching," Natalie said in a low voice.

Andi went back into the kitchen to check the screen door. The catch clicked firmly shut when she closed it. "I don't see how she could have got out through here," she whispered to Tristan.

"Maybe Mrs Giacomo didn't fasten it properly," he replied. "The wind might have blown it open just enough for Lola to squeeze through."

They went back to the living room. Tristan carefully wrote down details about the garden and the screen door in the red folder. Andi and Natalie exchanged a grin. Tris could be very serious about the detective stuff – but he had such a curiously good memory, he probably didn't need to write all this down, anyway.

"What does Lola eat?" asked Andi. Tristan and Natalie stared at her in surprise. "We might need to tempt her down from a tree, or out of a hiding place," she explained.

"She has a dry food mix," Mrs Giacomo said. "I'll get you some." She disappeared into the kitchen and came back with a plastic bag containing some food. "Here you are." Andi smiled as she took the bag. Mrs Giacomo was giving them a lot of helpful information that could lead them straight to Lola.

Natalie glanced around at the rows of certificates. "It looks like Lola wins lots of shows. That must mean she's pretty valuable. Do you think she might have been stolen?"

Mrs Giacomo gasped. "Oh, no! Surely not!" She swept Deena into her arms and hugged her tightly. "That would be terrible! Poor Lola!" Her eyes filled with tears. "And the poor kittens!"

"I'm sorry. I didn't mean to upset you," Natalie said hurriedly.

"It's all right. It's not your fault. I get upset all the time since Lola's disappeared." Mrs Giacomo dabbed her eyes with a tissue. "Losing your pet is the worst thing in the world."

"It is," Tristan agreed. "But Lola probably hasn't been stolen. She's more likely to have wandered off somewhere. Only a cat expert would know she was worth a lot of money. It's not like someone stealing snakes or lizards. Everyone knows they're worth loads."

"Yes, of course." Mrs Giacomo smiled weakly. "Is there anything else you need to know?"

"No, thanks," Natalie said. "You've given us a lot to get started with."

"We'll search around here first," Andi said. "Then, if we don't find Lola, we'll start putting up posters. We'll make flyers, too, and deliver them to every house nearby. Maybe Lola's got shut in a shed or something. We'll ask everyone to check." She smiled at Mrs Giacomo. "Don't worry, we'll find her."

"Oh, I hope so," Mrs Giacomo said. "Thank you for being so helpful."

They said goodbye and made their way slowly along the pavement, peering into gardens and under parked cars as they went. Every house in the road was different. Some were large and old with narrow windows and tall chimneys; others were smaller and more modern.

There was no sign of the missing cat anywhere, but if Lola wasn't used to being outside on her own, Andi knew she might have got scared and run a long way before looking for somewhere to hide.

A tall conifer stood at the end of the street. "What's that noise?" Natalie asked, stopping dead under the tree and clutching Tristan's arm.

"What noise?" said Tristan.

"Something rustling, up in the tree."

They peered up into the branches, listening. Sure enough, there it was again – a scratching from above. "It might be Lola!" Natalie whispered excitedly. "Maybe she's got stuck."

They gazed up, but the branches were too dense to see what was making the noise. "I'll climb up," Andi said. She grabbed the lowest branch and hauled herself into the tree.

"Are you sure this is a good idea?" Tristan said. "We don't want to have to stop the search to take you to hospital."

"I'll be fine," Andi said, stretching up for another handhold. The branches were strong enough to bear her weight, and she was a good climber. Soon, she was completely surrounded by pine needles. They blocked out most of the light and she felt as though she was inside a cool green cave. She stopped climbing to listen. For a moment there was no sound but the revving of a distant car. Then she heard a tiny scratching directly above her head. She peered up, but there was nothing to see but branches.

"Can you see her, Andi?" Natalie called.

"Not yet." Andi climbed on to the next branch. It was thinner than the last one and it creaked under her weight. She knew she wouldn't be able to go much higher; the branches wouldn't be strong enough to hold her as she neared the top of the tree. She hoped Lola hadn't climbed so high that she was out of reach.

Suddenly, there was a frantic scrambling sound above her head. A moment later, a squirrel scampered past her and darted down the other side of the trunk, into some shrubs around its base.

"Oh! It was only a squirrel!" Andi cried, disappointed.

"There's no way Lola could be up there, then," Tristan called. "A squirrel would never stay in a tree with a cat. You might as well come down, Andi."

Andi slid down again. "What a shame," she said, picking pine needles out of her hair. "I really thought we'd found her."

"Let's keep looking," Natalie said, brushing Andi's coat. "You'll have to take this to the dry cleaner's."

They turned the corner and found a small café on the next street. "I wonder if they've seen Lola,"

Andi said. "When Buddy was lost, a chef gave him a slice of pizza. Remember, Tris?"

"How could I forget? We found out about it straight after I'd been stuck in that hedge!"

"You were stuck in a hedge?" Natalie hooted with laughter. "I wish I'd been there to see it."

"I had to pull him out," Andi told her.

"You should have left him there."

Tristan folded his arms, pretending to be offended. "Remind me not to help *you* next time you get into trouble."

"Stop arguing, you two. Are you coming in or not?" asked Andi, pushing open the door of the café.

There were no customers, but a waitress was setting out knives and forks. "Sorry, we're not open yet," she said. "Can you come back in about half an hour?"

"We're looking for a lost cat," Tristan told her. "We wondered if she'd been here." He showed the waitress Lola's picture.

"No, though we had a little dog begging for scraps this morning. She was here yesterday, too."

"A dog?" Andi said.

"Yes, such a cutie! Cream-coloured and really friendly."

"Cream-coloured like porridge?" Natalie inquired. The waitress nodded, and Natalie looked at Andi. "You don't think . . . ?"

"It must be the dog we saw at the park," Andi said. She tore off the corner of a page from Tristan's folder and, ignoring his indignant look, scribbled her phone number on it. "If you see her again, could you call us, please? We're the Pet Finders Club and we help people who've lost their pets."

"What dog?" Tristan asked as they went out. "What's all this about? Are you two keeping secrets from ace detective Tristan Saunders?"

"We saw it yesterday," Andi told him. "It seemed to be on its own, but we couldn't tell for sure." She wished now that they'd tried harder: she didn't like to think of the poor dog running around, lonely and frightened. "We should keep a lookout for that dog, as well as Lola."

"You know what this means," Tristan said excitedly. He grinned at Andi and Natalie. "The Pet Finders Club has got two cases under investigation!"

Chapter Three

"What now?" Andi asked when they'd searched all along the next two roads without seeing any sign of Lola.

"We'd better start on the posters," Natalie suggested. "The sooner we let people know that Lola's missing, the sooner we'll find her."

"First, I want to go back and talk to Mrs Giacomo again," Tristan said. "I'm beginning to think Natalie's idea that Lola might have been stolen could be right."

"But who'd steal a cat?" Andi asked. "I mean, she's Mrs Giacomo's *pet*."

"But she's a *valuable* pet," Tristan reminded her. "And a pregnant one, at that. Pedigree kittens sell for a lot of money."

Mrs Giacomo met them at the front door. "Have you found her?"

"Not yet," Andi admitted as they followed her into the living room and sat down. Deena jumped straight on to Tristan's lap and started kneading his leg with her front paws.

"What is it?" Mrs Giacomo asked anxiously, looking around at their solemn faces. "Is there something you're not telling me?"

"No," Andi said, as gently as she could. "Not really. But we're wondering about the chance that Lola *has* been stolen."

Mrs Giacomo nodded. "I've thought about that a bit more, too. It's a possibility."

"The thief would have to be someone who knows how valuable Lola is," Tristan pointed out, scratching the side of Deena's head. She rolled over, purring more loudly than ever, and he tickled her tummy.

"Is there someone in Aldcliffe who'd know about Russian Blues?" Natalie asked.

"Well, there's Paul Channing, of course. But there's no way he'd steal Lola. We're practically neighbours – he only lives in the next road – and he breeds Russian Blues, too."

Tristan entered Mr Channing's name in his folder, resting it on the arm of the sofa to avoid squashing Deena.

Andi spotted a newspaper clipping pinned to a board over a desk. "It says here that Lola won that trophy in a show in Lancaster, and that her show name is Princess Anastasia."

"That's right."

Deena began to chew the corner of Tristan's file, and he put his hand over it so that she licked his fingers instead. "Did Mr Channing enter a cat?" he asked.

"Well, yes. Two actually, but—"

"Aha!" Holding Deena back with his left hand, Tristan scribbled in the notebook again. "Did they win prizes?"

"Second and third. But really, I can't imagine . . ." Mrs Giacomo trailed off.

"How did Mr Channing seem when he found out his cats hadn't won?" asked Andi.

Mrs Giacomo was looking rather flustered. "He congratulated me. His cats, Snowdrop of the

Steppes and Beauty of Babylon, often come second or third to Lola. But if you're thinking Paul could be a thief – well, he just can't be. I've known him for years."

"Can you think of anyone else who might know that Lola's valuable?" Andi asked. Mrs Giacomo seemed so certain that Mr Channing couldn't be involved in Lola's disappearance, that they could well be following the wrong lead.

Mrs Giacomo shook her head. "Well, not in Aldcliffe. But people come to these shows from all over the country."

"That proves it, then," Tristan whispered to Andi. "If she's been stolen, this Mr Channing must have done it."

"It doesn't prove anything, Tristan," she hissed back. "For starters, why would Mr Channing have waited until now to take Lola, when she often beats his cats into second place? Unless he was after the kittens, of course . . ."

"We've got to make those posters," interrupted Natalie.

"Thanks again for helping," Mrs Giacomo said, as they headed for the door. "If you need to know anything else, just give me a ring."

"We will," Andi promised.

They hurried down the driveway. "It's obvious where Lola is," Tristan said as they closed the gate behind them. "Mr Channing's got her."

"We don't know that," Andi said.

"I do. Who stands to gain the most from Lola disappearing?"

"Mr Channing. Possibly. But that doesn't make him a thief," Andi argued. "Mrs Giacomo doesn't think he's done it."

"He's the most likely person to have taken her. I bet he secretly hates Mrs Giacomo because her cat wins more prizes than his. We should go over to his house right now and look round." Tristan shoved the file into his backpack, looking very determined.

"We can hardly break in," Natalie pointed out. "We haven't got a search warrant, and I'm not going to try out the police again after our last case."

Andi cringed at the thought of how dangerously they'd acted while rescuing Christine's stolen animals. "Depending on what he does, he could be at work now, anyway."

Tristan grinned. "Perfect! He might have left a window open."

Andi and Natalie stared at him in disbelief. "You're not suggesting what I think you're suggesting, are you?" Natalie asked. "Even *you* couldn't be dim enough to want to break into Mr Channing's house."

"Definitely not!" Andi cried. "We'd get into loads of trouble for something like that. And there's no proof he took Lola. When Paws for Thought was robbed, we suspected all sorts of people who had nothing to do with it. We can't make the same mistake this time."

Natalie grabbed Andi's arm. "Come on. Let's go and make those posters and leave this idiot to get arrested on his own."

"Wait!" Tristan called, running after them. "OK, OK, I don't exactly want to break into his house, but you've got to admit he's our top suspect."

"He's a possibility," Natalie said. "And that's all. Now, are you coming with us, or should we get ready to visit you in prison?"

"I'll make the posters," Tristan muttered. "But

you're making a big mistake. Mr Channing's got Lola, I'm sure of it."

"That's it," Andi said, as the last of the flyers came spooling out of the printer. The Pet Finders were crammed into her mum's tiny study and Buddy was lying on Andi's feet, as he always did when she worked on the computer. Andi picked up a flyer and looked it over approvingly. Lola's sweet face gazed back at her.

"LOOKING FOR LOLA," Andi read out loud. "HAVE YOU SEEN THIS CAT? PLEASE CHECK SHEDS AND GARAGES." Her home phone and her mobile numbers were printed at the bottom, as usual.

"How many posters have we printed?" Natalie asked.

"Twenty," Andi replied. "And forty flyers."

"It's a waste of time and paper," Tristan grumbled, picking up the pile of posters and flapping them at Andi. "We all know who's got Lola. She'd be back with Mrs Giacomo by now if you'd listened to me."

"If you're so determined to investigate Mr

Channing, why don't you and Andi take some flyers, knock on all the doors in his road, and ask if anyone's seen a lost cat? Then, you can see how he reacts when you ask him about Lola."

"Aren't you coming with us?" Andi asked.

Natalie groaned. "I've got to go to the dentist!"

"Poor you," Andi sympathized.

Tristan looked much more cheerful. "That's a terrific idea!"

"What? Going to the dentist? I don't think so."

"No, knocking on doors. We might even be able to trick our way into Mr Channing's house."

"We don't know his address," Andi pointed out.

Tristan reached for the phone book. "It'll be in here." He flicked through the pages. "Channing, Channing . . . Here it is, Channing, P, 19 Windrush Drive."

"Windrush Drive?" Andi echoed. "Isn't that where Tangletree House is?"

"Yep." Tristan shut the phone book with a snap, making Buddy look up.

Andi bent down and patted him. "Let's take Buddy with us. And I don't want to be down there when it starts to get dark."

"Scared of the ghost?" Tristan said. "Because you're supposed to be the most sensible one of the three of us."

Natalie nudged him crossly with her elbow and Andi frowned. Being sensible sounded much too boring!

"Anyway," Tristan continued, "I passed Tangletree House a few days ago, when I was helping Dean with his paper round, and I didn't see or hear anything weird. Those stories are hoaxes." He looked disappointed, as if ghosts were almost as cool as snakes.

"Well, are we going, or what?" Andi cut in. She didn't want to think about Tangletree House. Buddy and Jet's reaction the other night had been pretty scary.

"Right." Tristan jumped up. "The sooner, the better, actually. My mum was complaining this morning that she never sees me these days, so I promised I'd be home early."

"She complained about never seeing you?" Natalie said, astonished. "Is she mad?"

"Come on, Bud," Tristan said, intentionally ignoring Natalie. "We're going cat-hunting."

Buddy leapt up, barking.

"Make sure you ring me if you find anything," Natalie said. "And wish me luck at the dentist."

"You won't need luck, you'll be fine," Andi said.

"As long as you like fillings and extractions," Tristan added.

Natalie threw a handful of paper clips at him.

"Here we are then," said Tristan, as he, Andi, and Buddy turned into Windrush Drive. "I know we really only want to speak to Mr Channing, but we need to look as though we're doing normal Pet Finders things. Let's put a poster on this lamppost." He pulled one out of his rucksack.

Andi looked along the road. The houses were mostly small, modern, and packed closely together. It seemed odd to think that Tangletree House – which was huge and old – stood on the same road, especially because Andi couldn't see it at all from here. It was set too far back from the pavement. "I hope people see the posters," she said. "This road looks very quiet."

They crossed over and hurried up the driveway of the first house.

41

"Don't talk for too long," Tristan warned as he rang the bell. "It's number 19 we want."

There was no answer to the doorbell. "Good!" Tristan said. "It'll speed things up if no one's in."

Andi pushed a flyer through the letter-box. "You might be wrong about Mr Channing, you know," she said.

"Wrong? Me? I don't think so." He suddenly looked serious. "We've got to find Lola, Andi. It's really important that we don't let Mrs Giacomo down."

Andi nodded, guessing that he was thinking about Lucy again.

There was nobody home at numbers 3 or 5, but a woman answered the door at number 7. "We're looking for a lost cat," Andi said, handing her a flyer. "Have you seen her?"

"No, sorry." She read the flyer. "But I'll check my garden and garage, and I'll call you if I find her."

"Here goes," Tristan said when they reached number 19. They could just see the chimneys of Tangletree House from here. The old house was at the far end of the street, and Andi tried not to look in that direction while they waited for Mr

Channing to open the door. To her relief, Buddy wasn't bothered about being near the house today. He was much more interested in sniffing around Mr Channing's front porch.

"I bet he can smell Lola," Tristan said. "I told you she—" He broke off as the door opened.

An exceptionally tall man smiled down at them. He was very smart-looking; his dark-brown hair was slicked back and he wore a grey suit with a pale green shirt and matching tie. "Hello," he said. "What can I do for you?" He suddenly noticed Buddy and his smile faded. "Keep that dog away," he snapped. "I've got cats in here."

Andi frowned. As if Buddy was likely to hurt his precious cats! She pulled Buddy close to her leg. "Sit, boy," she said. He flopped down at once and she patted him. "He won't go anywhere near your cats," she told Mr Channing, struggling to keep the irritation out of her voice.

"I'm glad to hear it," Mr Channing said. "And I'm glad he's well trained. I can't stand people who let their dogs roam around loose. Now, what do you want?"

"We're the Pet Finders Club and we're looking

for a lost cat," Tristan said, holding out one of the flyers. "Have you seen her?"

Mr Channing took the flyer and scanned it briefly. "Well, this cat looks a lot like my own, but I'm not missing any cats, nor have I seen any lost ones. Sorry."

"Yes, she's a Russian Blue," Andi said, nudging Tristan who was craning his neck to see past Mr Channing. It was obvious he was dying to get inside and poke around, but they couldn't let Mr Channing know that Tristan suspected him of being a cat-napper. "Her show name's Princess Anastasia," she added.

"Princess Anastasia?" Mr Channing echoed. He looked at the flyer again. "Of course it is. I recognize her now. She's Helen Giacomo's cat. Oh, poor Helen! She must be frantic with worry." He looked down at Tristan, who had leant so far into the hall that his rucksack was sweeping against Mr Channing's legs. "What are you doing?" he demanded.

Tristan turned bright red. "I . . . um . . . I was hoping to see one of your cats. I really love cats and I thought maybe you'd let me come in and see them."

"You can't possibly come inside. Not with that dog. I never allow dogs in my house."

"Andi and Buddy could wait outside—" Tristan began.

Before he could finish, there was a meow from inside the house. Buddy leapt forward, barking madly. "Stop it, Buddy!" Andi scolded, hauling on his lead to hold him back. "Bad boy!"

"Listen, I'm sorry but I don't know anything about this missing cat," Mr Channing said shortly. "So, please take your dog away now." He slammed the door shut.

"What an unfriendly man! Imagine not liking dogs!" Andi said as they walked away. "But I still don't think he's taken Lola. He seemed really upset when he realized it was Mrs Giacomo's cat we were searching for."

"Or he pretended to be."

"Oh, Tristan."

"I think he knows something. For a start, why didn't he recognize Lola right away? I bet he was just pretending not to know her because he's got her locked up."

"I don't know—" Andi began.

45

"And did you see how uncomfortable he looked when I asked if I could come in and see his cats? It was lucky for him Buddy barked when he did. That was a great excuse for keeping me out."

Andi stopped walking and stared at Tristan. "I suppose it does seem a bit suspicious."

"A bit!" Tristan exclaimed. "If you ask me, Mr Channing knows exactly what's happened to Lola!"

Chapter Four

It was nearly six o'clock when Andi said goodbye to Tristan.

"I'd better go and see my parents," he said, "in case they've forgotten what I look like. See you tomorrow."

"Time for a run, Bud," Andi said when Tristan had gone. If Mr Wallace, the teacher who ran the football team, was going to choose her to play in the next game, she needed to work on her fitness.

She began to jog along the pavement with Buddy scampering beside her. She took a longer route home than normal, but she managed to find her way easily. Although she'd only lived in Aldcliffe for a couple of months, she hardly ever got lost now – not like she had when she and her mum had first moved here.

"Almost home now, Bud," she said, spotting an unusual letterbox mounted on a post and painted with turquoise peacock feathers. The letterbox belonged to Mr Wheeler, who lived in the next road to hers.

Suddenly, Buddy jerked away. His lead slipped through Andi's fingers and he charged into Mr Wheeler's front garden.

"Buddy!" Andi yelled. "Come here!"

As he bounded across the lawn, trailing his lead, a small, whitish dog sprang out of some bushes and dashed up to him. Andi recognized the dog at once: it was the one she and Natalie had seen at the park.

The two dogs barked playfully, then darted round the side of the house. "Buddy, no!" Andi cried, hurtling after them.

Mr Wheeler was sitting in his back garden, with his back to Andi, dabbing paint on a canvas that was balanced on an artist's easel. He was wearing a bulky coat and a blue, woollen hat that almost hid his thick white hair.

"Mr Wheeler!" Andi called. "Look out!"

The old man glanced round just as the dogs reached him. Buddy dived under the easel, making it rock on its spindly wooden legs. Several tubes of paint, a palette knife, two paintbrushes, and a painty cloth tumbled on to the grass. The smaller dog circled Mr Wheeler, barking loudly, then shot forward, seized the cloth in her mouth, and darted away with it.

Mr Wheeler grabbed the easel to steady it.

"I'm so sorry, Mr Wheeler," Andi panted, running after Buddy. "Buddy saw that other dog in your front garden and he got away from me." The dogs were playing a tug-of-war game with the cloth in the middle of the lawn. "Stop it, Buddy!" Andi scolded. Darting towards him, she managed to grab the end of his lead. "Bad Buddy! Bad boy!"

Buddy's tail and ears drooped. He slunk towards her, aware that he'd misbehaved, and pressed himself against her legs.

"What are we going to do about the other one?" Mr Wheeler asked. The cream dog was rummaging around in a row of bushes near the road. "I don't want to risk picking her up, in case she gets scared. Most dogs are perfectly safe, but you never know."

"I've got some of Buddy's dog treats in my pocket," Andi said. "You might be able to catch her with those." She threw the bag to Mr Wheeler.

He tossed one on to the lawn a little way in front of the strange dog. She trotted over to it, her tail wagging. She wolfed down the treat, then looked hopefully at Mr Wheeler with her head to one side.

"She looks as though she's got a bit of Border terrier in her," Andi said, admiring her cute, boxy head and pricked ears.

"I think you're right," Mr Wheeler agreed. He threw another dog treat. "Here, girl."

The dog ran to it and gobbled it up. "She likes these," Mr Wheeler said as the little dog jumped up and planted her paws on his knee.

The old man let her sniff his hand, then he stroked her. She squirmed with pleasure, her tail wagging hard. "What a friendly little thing!" he said. "I wonder who she belongs to."

"I think she's lost," Andi said. She told Mr Wheeler about seeing the dog in the park.

"So, what will you do with her now?" he asked.

"I could take her home with me while we try to find her owner," Andi suggested.

"You come along with me then, young lady," said Mr Wheeler, patting the lost dog, "and I'll find you a temporary lead." He went indoors with the dog trotting at his heels. A moment later they reappeared with a piece of thick string twisted through the dog's collar. "This string should last until you get her home."

"Thanks." Andi retrieved the cloth that the dogs had been playing with and picked up the paintbrushes. "What a great picture!" she said. Mr Wheeler was painting the trees at the end of his garden in their autumn colours.

"Thanks. The trees are so lovely this year that I just had to get out here and paint." Mr Wheeler handed her the makeshift lead, then sat down at his easel again. "I think I've got time for a few more leaves before the light goes."

"See you later." Andi led the two dogs around the side of the house and headed for home. They trotted beside her, nuzzling each other, their tails wagging furiously. "Anyone would think you two had known each other for years!" Andi laughed. "You must like making friends as much as I do, Bud!"

* * *

Mrs Talbot was in the kitchen when Andi came in with the two dogs. "Who's this?" she asked, looking down at the visitor in surprise.

"I'm going to call her Oat," Andi said, "because of her colour – a bit like porridge, don't you think? She's lost and we need to find her owner."

"You'd better take her to the RSPCA," said Mrs Talbot. She glanced at the clock on the wall. "But it will be closed now, so she'll have to stay with us tonight." She laughed. "I don't know! You three started out as the Pet Finders Club but now you seem to be going into the pet hotel business, as well!"

Andi grinned. That sounded pretty cool to her.

Natalie and Tristan arrived at Andi's house just before nine o'clock the next morning. Andi had called to tell them about Oat the evening before.

"What a sweetie!" Natalie said, as Oat squirmed around her legs, her tail wagging.

"She seems pretty healthy," Tristan said, as the little dog jumped up at him, "so she can't have been lost for long."

"What should we do with her?" Natalie asked.

"Mum thinks we should take her to the RSPCA," Andi said. "They're open on Saturday mornings."

"They've got a microchip scanner, too," Tristan added. "So if Oat's been chipped we'll find out who her owner is straight away – like we did with Jet, remember?"

They may have been lucky with microchips once before, but Andi didn't want to get her hopes up too high this time. She tried to think about other things while her mum drove them to the RSPCA centre, but then all she could think about was Agnes Delaney's ghost.

"I'll wait in the car," Mrs Talbot offered when they arrived. "I'm not sure there'll be room for all of us in there."

The Pet Finders hurried inside the RSPCA building with Oat. Fisher Pearce, the resident vet, and friend to Christine Wilson, came out to meet them. "Hello! Caught any thieves recently?" he joked as he showed them into his consulting room. "Who's this?"

"We call her Oat," Andi told him. "She's lost. We thought she might be microchipped."

"Let's hope she is." Fisher lifted Oat on to the

table and ran a handheld scanner over the fur on her neck. "No luck, I'm afraid," he said, when the green light didn't flash. "And we've had no reports of lost dogs lately. Looks like it's the kennel for you, girl." He rubbed Oat's chest and she licked his hand.

"I could look after her for now while we try to track down her owner," Andi suggested. Oat was so cute, she didn't like to think of her being in an unfamiliar kennel.

Fisher looked thoughtful. "Have you asked your mum about this?"

"Not yet. But I'm sure she won't mind. She's outside in the car now. I could run out and ask her."

"OK," Fisher agreed. "You do that, while I give Oat a quick check-up."

Andi raced outside. "Mum, you've got to let me keep Oat while we try to find her owner, okay? Please? She's not microchipped, so she'd have to stay in the kennels otherwise."

Mrs Talbot smiled. "I don't see why not. She's adorable, and she and Buddy are the best of friends already."

"Oh, thank you!" Andi hugged her mum, then

ran back inside. "She said yes!" she announced, bursting into the consulting room.

Fisher lifted Oat down from the table. "That's great," he said. "Now let me find a lead to lend you. You'll never be able to take her for walks on this string." He opened a cupboard and began to rummage through the shelves. "What other cases are you Pet Finders working on at the moment?"

"We're looking for a missing Russian Blue cat," Natalie told him.

Fisher looked around in surprise. "A Russian Blue? That's funny. I was at Paul Channing's house this morning delivering some Russian Blue kittens. His regular vet, Dr Harvey, is on holiday. Poor man, he's probably the most anxious pet owner I've ever met! Phoned me three times on Thursday to tell me how his cat was doing, and four times yesterday." He dived into the cupboard again. "Still, it all ended happily. The kittens are beautiful."

Tristan nudged Andi in the ribs. "See?" he hissed. "Those kittens have got to be Lola's!"

Chapter Five

"Let's walk home," Natalie suggested. "Your mum won't mind going back without us, will she, Andi?"

"I don't think so." Andi left Natalie holding Oat on her new lead and ran to the car. "Is it okay if we walk back, Mum?"

"Of course. It'll give me a chance to do some shopping. I'll see you at home later." Mrs Talbot drove away.

"Fisher's news proves it," Tristan said, as Andi joined him and Natalie again. "Mr Channing's got a cat with kittens. He *has* to be the thief."

Andi wasn't so sure. "Maybe it's just a coincidence. Both cats might have been expecting kittens at the same time."

"Come off it," Tristan argued. "Lola is at Mr

Channing's and we've got to find a way to get in there."

"What about Oat?" Andi asked, to change the subject. She had a bad feeling that Tristan might march over to Mr Channing's house right now and barge inside.

Oat gave a bark as if to say she wished they'd hurry up and get her home.

"We could make posters with DO YOU KNOW THIS DOG? at the top, and a picture of Oat underneath," Natalie suggested.

"Good idea!" Tristan agreed. "It's lucky—" He broke off suddenly. "Hey, there's a shop over there. I could do with a snack."

"You can't be hungry!" Andi exclaimed. "Didn't you have any breakfast?"

"Breakfast was ages ago." He darted across the road and into the shop. He came out a moment later with a muesli bar and a copy of the local newspaper.

"I've just realized something. Papers have a classified ad section."

"So?"

"I know what Tris means," said Andi. "Somebody might be advertising in it if they've lost Oat!" She took the paper and flicked through it until she found the right page. "Here!"

They all crowded around to see. There were adverts selling goldfish and baby hamsters, but nobody had lost a dog. Then Tristan suddenly stabbed the page with an accusing finger. "There! Look! Russian Blue kittens for sale. And the phone number has an Aldcliffe area code. It must be Mr Channing."

"They can't be Lola's," Natalie said. "Mr Channing wouldn't be daft enough to advertise a stolen cat's kittens."

"Someone would find out and he'd be arrested," Andi added.

"But now we'll have an excuse to go into his house. We can pretend that one of us wants to buy a kitten. That way we'll get to see the mother," Tristan said, exasperated. "Don't you care about finding Lola? Mrs Giacomo's going out of her mind with worry and you two just keep insisting that Mr Channing hasn't got her."

"Of course we care," Andi said. "But there's no proof that Mr Channing's taken her. We have to think of other possibilities, too, Tristan."

"Such as?"

Andi and Natalie looked at each other. The posters hadn't inspired any calls yet, and their search hadn't turned up any clues. "OK," Andi sighed. "There's no harm in looking at the kittens' mother, I suppose. And if she does turn out to be Lola, then that will be another case solved."

Natalie took out her mobile phone. "I'll ring now and make an appointment." She punched in the number.

They waited impatiently for someone to answer, then Natalie gave them a thumbs-up. "Hello," she said. "I saw your advert for kittens and I'd like to come and see them. My parents are thinking of buying me a kitten for my birthday."

There was a pause while Natalie listened.

"She sounds lovely," she said. "What's the address? Okay, I'll see you later, then. Thanks!" She switched off her phone. "It's Mr Channing's ad, all right. That was his wife. She says the mother cat is called Snowdrop of the Steppes."

"More like Lola!" Tristan snorted.

"I'm going over there this afternoon at half past one," Natalie continued.

"Great," Andi said.

"Half past one?" Tristan echoed.

"What's wrong with that?"

"I'm helping out at Paws for Thought. Couldn't you have made the appointment for later? I'll be finished by four o'clock."

"Sorry, that was the only time Mr and Mrs Channing had free," Natalie said.

"You'll be able to ask Christine's customers about Oat, Tristan," Andi pointed out. "Maybe one of them will know someone who's lost a dog."

Tristan shrugged. "I suppose so." He bent down to stroke the little dog's head. "Don't worry, girl. We'll find out where you're from soon."

Andi and Natalie met outside Mr Channing's house just before one thirty. Natalie was dressed in a pair of faded jeans and a beaded pink top that Andi had seen in the window of a boutique in the high street. "You look great," she said.

"I thought I'd better look as though my parents have plenty of money. Russian Blue kittens are probably expensive. Do you like this top?"

"Love it." Andi fingered the row of beads that ran

round the edge of the sleeve. "But the jeans look a bit old."

"Old! I only bought them last week. They're the latest style!"

"Sorry," Andi laughed. "Come on, we'd better go in." She glanced along the road towards the chimneys of Tangletree House and shivered.

Mr Channing opened the door to them. "Hello," he said. He looked at Andi in surprise. "Aren't you the girl who came here looking for Princess Anastasia?"

Andi froze, then thought fast. "Oh, yeah! That's right. Isn't it funny that my friend wants to buy one of your kittens?"

"Uh, yes, but I hope you haven't brought your dog with you."

"No, he's at home."

Andi and Natalie followed Mr Channing inside. They crossed a cluttered hallway, dodging a shopping basket, two sports bags and a pair of battered jogging shoes. Then Mr Channing ushered them into a cosy living room with a fire crackling in the hearth. A cat lay in a basket beside the fire with four tiny grey kittens curled up next to her. Two were the same silver-grey as their mother, one was a bit darker with silver-tipped ears, and the fourth was the colour of the sky on a rainy day.

"Oh, they're so cute!" Natalie exclaimed, as if she'd forgotten she was only pretending to be interested. She knelt beside the basket and picked up the darkest kitten. It gave a tiny purr, then snuggled down in her hands.

"You do realize that they won't be able to leave their mother for another eight weeks?" Mr Channing said.

"Yes. But that will be OK," Natalie replied. "I don't mind waiting."

"I'll leave you to get to know them," Mr Channing said. "I'll be in the kitchen if you need me. The mother's called Snowdrop." He went out.

Andi took out the photo of Lola. Mr Channing's cat was much paler, but her face was disturbingly similar, with the same wide, green eyes and friendly expression. "I don't think this can be Lola," she said, peering closely at the cat in the basket.

Natalie didn't reply. She was holding the kitten next to her face and stroking it with one finger.

"Nat!" Andi shoved the photo under Natalie's nose. "What do you think? Is this cat Lola?"

"Oh, sorry. This kitten is so sweet!"

"We've come to look at the mother," Andi reminded her.

Natalie frowned at the photo, then looked at the cat. "Her fur's paler than Lola's."

"That's what I thought," Andi said. "Tristan was wrong about this."

"Unless Mr Channing's dyed her."

"Dyed her? Can you dye cats?"

"I don't see why not. People have their hair dyed all the time. What's the difference?"

Andi admitted that Nat had a point. She bent over the basket and rubbed the cat's fur, flattening it down until she could see right to the end of some of the hairs. If she'd been dyed, there'd be a trace of darker fur close to her skin where the hairs were growing out. The cat began to purr and pressed her head against Andi's sleeve.

"Can you see anything?" Natalie asked.

"Her fur's pale all the way through. She's definitely not Lola. We were right all along. Mr Channing hasn't got anything to do with Lola's disappearance." She picked up the smallest kitten and held it against her chest. The tiny creature felt like it was made of feathers. "I wish you were really buying one, Nat," Andi whispered. "They're adorable."

"Me too."

Andi began to feel uncomfortably hot being so close to the fire. "I'm boiling," she complained. "I'm just going to ask Mr Channing for a glass of water, then we should go."

"What are we going to say about the kittens?"

"Say you'll think it over." Andi carefully put the kitten back in the basket and watched, enchanted, as it snuggled against its mother's side again. "I won't be long." She went out into the hall, shutting the living-room door behind her so the kittens couldn't get out.

At the end of the hall, the door was ajar and Andi could hear Mr and Mrs Channing talking in the kitchen.

"I don't know what to do," Mr Channing was saying.

"Well, I think you should tell that girl what you saw," his wife replied.

Andi gasped. Was Mrs Channing talking about her? She crept closer, feeling like a spy.

"How can I?" Mr Channing demanded. "I've already told her and her friend that I don't know anything."

Andi's heart began to pound. Mr Channing had been lying all along. He *did* know something about Lola's disappearance!

Chapter Six

"I'm going to go and see how the girls are getting on with the kittens," Mr Channing said, his voice getting louder as if he was moving towards the door.

Andi darted back along the hall and burst into the living room.

Natalie looked up in astonishment. "What's happened?"

"I can't tell you now." Andi quickly shut the door. Then she flung herself down beside the basket of kittens and began to stroke the one nearest to her.

Mr Channing came in. "Have you decided which one you'd like?"

"Not yet," Natalie sighed, picking up a different kitten. "I think I need a bit longer. They're all so gorgeous."

Andi flashed her a horrified look. "We've got to go," she mouthed, keeping her back towards Mr Channing.

"Actually," Natalie said hastily, catching Andi's look, "I ought to talk to my parents about which one to have, too." She put the kitten she was holding back into the basket and stood up.

"Don't take too long to decide, or I might have sold them all," warned Mr Channing. "Russian Blues are very popular."

"I won't." Natalie looked back wistfully at the kittens as Mr Channing showed them out into the hall. Another Russian Blue cat was coming down the stairs. Andi stared at it, wondering if it could be Lola. "You've got two cats," she said.

"That's right. This is Beauty."

Andi clicked her fingers and the cat ran to her. She stroked it, but she could see, now that it was close to her, that it couldn't possibly be Lola. It was much too big. Mrs Giacomo had said Lola was a small cat.

"What was all that about?" Natalie demanded, when the front door closed behind them.

"Wait until we're away from the house," Andi whispered dramatically.

As they came out of the front garden, they saw Tristan flying down the pavement towards them. "How did it go?" he called. He jumped off his skateboard and snatched it up before the wheels stopped spinning.

"What are you doing here?" said Andi. "I thought you were helping out at Paws for Thought."

"I was, but Christine let me go early. Did you find Lola?"

"No, but Mr Channing definitely knows something." Andi told them what she'd overheard as they walked away from the house.

"It doesn't sound as though he's cat-napped Lola himself," Natalie said thoughtfully. "But he obviously saw something important."

"I bet he knows exactly where Lola is," Tristan insisted. "We should go back right now and ask him to tell us everything."

"He'd only lie," Natalie pointed out. "He'd probably say Andi misheard and that he wasn't talking about Lola at all."

"Or he'd yell at us for spying on him," Andi added.

"But we've got to do something!" Tristan argued. "Mrs Giacomo is relying on us to find Lola."

"I know," Andi said. "I'm worried about Lola, too. But there's no point asking Mr Channing. We'll have to think of another way to find out what he saw."

"Come back to my house so we can talk about it," Tristan said.

It was nearly half past two when they arrived at Tristan's house. Dean, Tristan's fifteen-year-old brother, was coming down the stairs listening to his Ipod. "Hey," he said, pushing the headphones down around his neck. "What's wrong?"

Tristan told him what Andi had overheard at Mr Channing's house. "We think he must have seen Lola somewhere."

"Sounds like it," Dean agreed. "What are you gonna do about it?"

"We were hoping to come up with some more ideas about that," Andi admitted.

"We've searched everywhere we can think of," Tristan added gloomily. "We've been down every road, looked under every parked car . . ."

Dean sat down on the stairs, frowning thoughtfully. "So you don't think Lola's hiding near Mr Channing's house?"

"No."

"He might have seen her somewhere else, then. Maybe she wandered further than you thought. Maybe he spotted her on his way home from somewhere."

"Of course!" Natalie burst out. "We just need to work out where he goes regularly. Then we can follow his route and look for possible hiding places. That's a great idea, Dean!"

Dean grinned at her from under a wisp of his spiky blond hair. Natalie turned bright red and fiddled with her friendship bracelet.

"I think it's a stupid idea," Tristan said. "We don't know where Mr Channing works, or does his shopping, or anything."

"We might be able to find out, though," Andi pointed out.

Dean agreed. "You should think yourself lucky, Tris, to have a brother with good looks *and* brains." Laughing, he went along the hall and out into the back garden.

"Good looks!" Tristan hooted. "Brains! He must be joking."

Andi grinned. "I know someone who thinks he's good-looking." She looked pointedly at Nat.

"You've got a crush on my brother?" Tristan said, staring at Natalie. "Are you mad?"

Natalie glared at him. "It's none of your business who I like, Tristan! And if—"

"So how are we going to find out where Mr Channing works?" Andi interrupted before they started another round of bickering.

"We can't follow him from his house if he drives his car most of the time," Tristan pointed out. "Not even *you* could run fast enough to keep up with a car, Andi."

"Fisher might know where he works," Natalie said. "He's probably got all of Mr Channing's contact details after helping with Snowdrop's kittens, you know, his work phone number and everything."

"That's right!" Tristan noted, seemingly having forgiven Natalie for liking his brother. Then his face fell. "But how can we ask him? He'll want to know why we need the information. He might think we were plotting something, like when we found our last thief's hideout."

They moved into the kitchen. Andi and Natalie sat on stools at the breakfast bar while Tristan poured orange juice into three glasses. They sipped their drinks in silence, thinking hard.

At last, Andi spoke up. "What about Oat? We mustn't forget her. Did you have any luck finding her owner, Tristan?"

"No." He set down his glass. "I bet, if nobody knows anything about her, that she came from out of town. Maybe she just walked here."

"I don't think so." Andi shook her head. "Her paws weren't sore and she looked well-fed."

"Yeah, but she might have stopped at cafés, though, like Buddy did," Natalie reminded her.

"Perhaps she belongs to someone who was visiting Aldcliffe?" Tristan suggested.

"I hope not," Andi said. "If she does, then putting up posters won't help, because her owner won't be around to see them."

"Then we'll need to find a new way of tracking lost owners," Natalie said. "But we haven't even made the posters yet. Let's go over to your house now and get working on them."

After school on Monday afternoon, the Pet Finders
met to walk their dogs. Andi had brought Buddy
and Oat, Natalie had Jet, and Tristan had borrowed
Christine's cocker spaniel, Max.

The four dogs rushed up to each other, barking
excitedly. "Whoa, Jet!" Natalie shrieked as the
excited black Labrador almost pulled her over. She
regained her balance. "Sometimes I wonder why I
like dogs!"

"Because they're cute and cuddly," Andi said,
giving Buddy an affectionate pat.

As they headed for the park, they passed one of
the posters they'd made for Oat. They had stuck
twenty of them to lampposts in the roads
surrounding the park the day before. "That's you,
Oat!" Andi said, stopping to look at it. She sighed.
"I wish somebody would phone and claim you."

Just then, a lorry came rumbling along the road.
At once, Oat pulled towards it, whining.

"What's she doing?" Andi asked, puzzled. They
stopped to watch as Oat strained towards the lorry.
But when it sped by, she sank down dejectedly on
the pavement.

"What's wrong with her?" said Natalie.

Andi crouched beside her. "I don't know." She stroked Oat's head, but the little dog didn't even look at her. "Come on, Oat," Andi coaxed. "Cheer up, girl." She looked anxiously at Natalie and Tristan. "I haven't seen her like this before. Do you think she's ill?"

Buddy trotted over. He licked Oat's face, then nudged her with his nose as though he were trying to make her stand up.

Oat turned her head away with a mournful sigh.

A second lorry appeared. At once, the little dog leapt up. She began to bark eagerly, her strange mood forgotten. But once the lorry had passed them, she slumped down again.

"It's the lorries that are making her act like this," Andi said. "Do you think she's frightened of the noise they make?"

"She could be," Tristan said. "Come on. Let's not hang around if they're upsetting her."

They pulled Oat to her feet and walked on. Several cars sped by, but Oat didn't notice them at all.

"Not all the traffic's bothering her," Natalie

remarked. "She's not even *looking* at the cars."

A furniture lorry approached. As expected now, Oat halted, quivering with excitement, then strained towards the lorry, pulling so hard against her lead that Andi's fingers went numb. Tristan grabbed the lead too. "It's all right, girl," he said. "It's only a lorry."

"You know what?" said Natalie, looking down at Oat. "She's not scared at all. It looks as though she's really *happy* to see the lorries."

The third lorry rumbled past and Oat sank down again as if she'd lost her favourite toy and a juicy bone all at once.

Andi got an idea then. "Maybe she came to Aldcliffe in a lorry?" she suggested. "Could she have been trapped in a removal van or delivery lorry without anyone noticing? I've heard of that happening to cats."

Tristan shook his head. "Wouldn't she be afraid of lorries then? She'd think they were going to take her away again. No, I think she's used to riding in lorries because ... because ..." He trailed off.

"Because her owner's a lorry driver!" Natalie

finished triumphantly, holding up her hand for a high five.

"So maybe she was left behind when he made a delivery to a shop or something!" Andi said.

"But there are loads of shops in Aldcliffe," Tristan pointed out. "We can't go to every one to ask if anyone recognizes her. It'll take years."

"Why don't we go back to where we first saw her in the park?" suggested Natalie. "That might lead to some clues."

Tristan took Buddy's lead and Andi picked Oat up. The little dog was too miserable to even walk. Andi hugged her tight, trying to make her feel better. "We'll find your owner soon, Oat," she promised.

As soon as they reached the park, Tristan let Buddy and Max off their leads. They raced away, then circled back and barked at Oat. She lifted her head from Andi's shoulder and squirmed to be put down. "Don't let her off her lead," Natalie warned. "We don't want her dashing off again."

"Come on," Andi said. "Let's run." Holding tight to Oat's lead, she sprinted across the grass with Oat running beside her and Buddy and Max hard on her heels. She headed in the direction of the woods, then veered off to the right, trying to remember exactly where she and Natalie had been when they'd first spotted Oat. She reached a clump of bushes and stopped to look back. Tristan and Natalie were a long way behind. "Hurry up!" she yelled.

They reached her at last, panting hard. "It's all right for you," Tristan puffed. "You're a star football player and a runner, but some of us have got less energetic hobbies."

Andi laughed. "You should come jogging with me, Tristan. And you too, Natalie."

"No, thanks," Natalie said firmly. "I think I'll stick to chess."

"Is this the place where you first saw Oat?" Tristan asked.

"I think so," Andi said.

"No, it was further over," Natalie said, "past that tree over there."

Andi looked where she was pointing. "No, it wasn't. We came round the pond and headed for the woods." She caught sight of a cluster of thorny, leafless bushes with a few shrivelled roses attached.

"There!" she said. "Those rose bushes. We walked right past them. I remember catching my coat on a thorn."

"Yeah, but we crossed a path, too," Natalie said. "And there's no path near the roses so . . ."

"Oat, no!" Andi yelled.

Oat had jerked free while they had been busy arguing. She raced away, trailing her lead behind her.

"Come back!" Tristan shouted.

They sped after her. Andi soon left Tristan and Natalie a long way behind, but the distance between her and Oat was growing wider by the second. She was afraid she wouldn't catch up and that the little dog would be lost again.

Buddy darted along beside Andi, his little legs pumping furiously. Andi pushed herself harder than ever, but Oat just seemed to move even quicker. Suddenly, to Andi's relief, Oat reached a path and stopped. She began to sniff along the ground as though she was trying to work out the right way to go.

"Oat!" Andi panted, slowing a little. "Here, girl."

The little dog looked up and wagged her tail.

Andi stopped running. She approached Oat cautiously, worried that she might take off again.

Oat went on sniffing, occasionally lifting her head to sneak a glance at Andi. As soon as she was close enough, Andi grabbed her lead. "Don't you run off again," she scolded, ruffling Oat's ears. She looked around and saw Natalie and Tristan sauntering towards her. "Don't hurry, will you?" she called sarcastically.

"We didn't want to spoil your fun," Tristan said. "You're always saying you need to work out more, and that seemed like a perfect opportunity."

"We didn't want to overtake you and show you up," Natalie added, nudging Tristan.

"We were trying to work out where we were when we first saw Oat," Andi reminded them sternly. "And I still think we were somewhere near those rose bushes."

Natalie opened her mouth to argue but before she could speak, Tristan cut in. "Don't start arguing again. It doesn't matter where *you* were standing when you saw Oat. What matters is where *she* was."

Andi nodded. "I suppose you're right."

"Don't tell him that," Natalie groaned. "He'll go on about it for days."

Andi looked round. "This is where we saw her," she said. "She was running along this path. Then she disappeared into that patch of shrubbery. Clever girl, Oat! She must have known what we were saying. Where does the path go, Tristan? Are there any shops this way that a lorry would deliver to?"

"No, this path just leads to the road out of town."

Natalie sighed. "I really thought we were on to something there."

"Wait. We still might be!" Andi turned to Tristan. "Where do lorries stop in Aldcliffe? You know, when the drivers need food and stuff."

He frowned. "There are a few places. There's a café on Half Mile Lane and one on Belvedere Road. Oh, and there's also an overnight lorry park on Stratton Street."

"Which one's closest to here?"

"Half Mile Lane." Tristan smiled. "And this path runs really close to it. You might be on to something, Andi."

"Careful," Natalie warned. "We don't want Andi getting a swollen head, too."

Andi laughed. "You're just jealous because you didn't think of it yourself."

"Come on!" Tristan whooped. "What are we waiting for?"

Andi shot away at first, then slowed to a jog to allow the others to catch up with her. It wouldn't be fair if she found Oat's owner by herself, but she was impatient to reach the lorry stop. It would be fantastic to see Oat reunited with her owner.

The café at the rest stop was a one-storey concrete building set in the middle of a vast parking area. Lorries of all sizes, from enormous juggernauts with double trailers, to small delivery vans, were parked all around.

"This place is certainly popular," Andi said. "I wonder if Oat's owner is here now."

A burly man came out of the café then, wiping his fingers on a paper towel. He glanced at them, then stopped and stared. "Apple?" he exclaimed. "Apple? Is that you?"

Oat gave a bark of recognition and lurched forward. Her lead slipped through Andi's fingers yet again as she charged across the tarmac towards the man.

Tristan grinned triumphantly and gave Andi a high five. "Looks like the Pet Finders have just closed another case!"

Chapter Seven

"Where did you find her?" the man called, as Oat leapt around him.

"In the park a couple of days ago," Andi replied. "She's been staying with me while we tried to track you down. We're the Pet Finders Club." She beamed at the man. "I suppose we can stop looking now."

"Oh, no," the man said. "Apple's not *my* dog. She belongs to Pete, one of the Sun-Fruit drivers." He bent down to pick up the end of her lead and she jumped up to lick his cheek. "You rascal," he laughed, rubbing her head.

"Not yours!" Natalie said with disbelief. "I don't suppose Pete's here now, is he?"

The man glanced around the lorry park. "I can't

see his rig. And I don't know how to get in touch with him, either, I'm afraid. We just share a table sometimes when we meet up here." He handed the lead to Andi. "I'd love to help you find him, but I've got to go. Otherwise, I'll have my boss breathing down my neck."

"Uh, OK. Thanks for telling us about Pete," said Tristan.

"Did he say Pete drove for Sun-Fruit?" Natalie asked, as his lorry drove away.

"That's right," Andi replied.

Natalie pointed to the main road that ran past the lorry stop. "There's a Sun-Fruit lorry now."

They raced across the parking area towards the lorry, waving and yelling, but the driver roared past without stopping. "There's a phone number on the side!" Andi yelled. "Quick, has anyone got a pen?"

"Don't worry about it, I've got it!" Tristan said, as the lorry disappeared around the corner. "My head is bursting with information, and the Sun-Fruit phone number and address are in there now, too."

"I don't believe you," Natalie said. "I know you think you're some sort of memory man, but nobody could remember a phone number they saw that quickly. And the address was written in really tiny letters."

Tristan shrugged, then recited the number and the address off the top of his head.

"You're amazing," Andi gasped.

They hurried back to Andi's house to phone Sun-Fruit. "Keep hold of that number, Tristan," she urged, as they raced over her lawn to the front door. Andi couldn't help getting her hopes up this time. All the information they'd stumbled on in the last hour was simply too much to let them down.

"I won't forget it," promised Tristan. "I think I know my own brain better than you do."

They crowded through the Talbots' front door and into the hallway, where Andi grabbed the phone. "OK, what was it?" she asked hurriedly.

Tristan recited the number while Andi dialled, though he paused a few times to pretend he'd lost it. When she'd finally entered the number in its entirety, it was only a moment before her call was answered. "Sun-Fruit. How may I help you?"

"Hello," Andi said. "I've found a dog called Apple

and I think it belongs to one of your drivers. His name's Pete."

"Oh, how wonderful!" the receptionist cried. "Pete will be so relieved! He's been terribly worried about Apple. Is she all right?"

"She's fine," Andi said.

"That's such good news! Give me your address, and I'll call Pete on his mobile to tell him the dog's safe."

Andi gave her address.

"Pete's only about twenty minutes from there now," the lady said. "I'll tell him to come straight over."

Andi beamed at Tristan and Natalie as she hung up the receiver. "He's on his way," she said. "Do you hear that, Oat – or Apple? Your owner's coming for you!"

Apple rolled over so that Andi could stroke her tummy, then she leapt up, raced up the stairs and down again, and finally shot into the living room with the other dogs tearing behind her.

"Let's go and tell my mum the good news," Andi said, heading for the kitchen.

* * *

Pete was a huge grizzly bear of a man, with a bushy beard and a crinkly-eyed smile. The moment Andi opened the door to him, Apple leapt into his arms and he hugged her tightly. The little dog almost disappeared in his giant hands. "Apple! Where have you been? I thought you'd gone for good, girl."

"Come in," Andi said, feeling a bit shy.

Pete followed her into the living room where Natalie and Tristan were waiting. Buddy, Jet, and Max were dozing on the sofa in a tangle of furry legs and tails.

"Thank you so much for finding her for me," Pete said. He sat down and Apple squirmed on to his lap, licking his face, his hands, his ears . . .

"It's what we do," Tristan explained. "We're the Pet Finders Club."

"Really? So you gather up lost pets and find their owners?"

"Yes. And owners call us if they've lost a pet, too, so we can track it down."

"What a great idea!" Pete said. "It's lucky Apple chose to jump out of my lorry in Aldcliffe, of all places. We might not have been so lucky if you three hadn't found her."

"How did she get lost?" Andi asked.

"She was asleep in my cab when I stopped at Half Mile Lane. There's a ledge behind the driver's seat and she curls up there sometimes for a nap." He broke off, laughing, as Apple licked his nose. "It was a sunny day," he continued, "and it was hot in my cab, so I left the window open when I went into the café to get a coffee. When I came out, I didn't think to check on Apple. I just assumed she'd still be on her ledge, asleep."

"So she jumped out while you were in the café?" Natalie asked.

"Must have. When I got to my next stop, she wasn't there. I was horrified, I can tell you. But I couldn't turn back. You can't be late with fruit. It doesn't keep. You have to stick to your schedule." He hugged Apple again. "I've had a terrible few days, wondering where this little lady had gone to." He smiled at the Pet Finders. "You kids have been great! If it hadn't been for you . . ." He took out a large handkerchief and blew his nose. "Well, I might never have seen Apple again."

"We're glad you're back together again," Tristan

said, looking rather uncomfortable at Pete's display of emotion.

Pete put Apple down and stood up. "We'd better hit the road. I'm due back at the depot."

The Pet Finders stroked Apple one last time. "No more jumping out of windows," Andi warned.

"No chance of that," said Pete. "From now on, I'm just going to leave the windows open a crack for her." He shook hands with them all. "Thanks again for everything."

He opened the lorry door and helped tiny Apple jump in. She darted across to the passenger seat and stood with her front paws on the dashboard, her tongue lolling and her tail wagging furiously.

Pete climbed in after her, started the engine, and honked the horn at the kids. "Thanks!" he called out of the window as he drove away.

"I'm going to miss Apple," Andi sighed. It had been fun having two dogs, as well as a new best friend for Buddy to play with.

"Me, too," agreed Natalie.

"Buddy will be sorry she's gone," Andi added.

"Yeah, but he'll get his basket all to himself again," Tristan pointed out. "And we've solved another case. I think this calls for a celebration smoothie. Anyone up for the Banana Beach Café? You never know, we might see Fisher. Maybe we'll come up with some way of finding out where Mr Channing works."

The Banana Beach Café was one of Andi's favourite places in Aldcliffe. The building was painted brilliant yellow and the tables outside had rainbow-coloured sun umbrellas that brightened up the place, even when the sky was grey. It was run by Maggie and Jango Pearce, Fisher's mum and dad.

Andi and Tristan left Natalie sitting outside on a bench with the dogs, while they went inside to order. "Say hello to Long John for me," she called after them.

Long John Silver, a beautiful green-and-blue parrot, was strutting along the counter. "Bananas!" he squawked as they walked in.

"Hello, Long John," Andi said, stroking the parrot's feathery chest.

The parrot rubbed his head against her hand. "Bananas!" he repeated. "More bananas!"

"Hello, Tristan! Hello, Andi!" Maggie Pearce

cried, hurrying out of the back room so that the beaded curtain covering the doorway rattled madly. "Jango! Look who it is!" She was a beaming, round-faced Jamaican woman, and today, as usual, she wore a dress the colour of sunflowers. She was carrying a milk jug that she set down on the counter.

"Hi, Maggie," said Tristan.

"Hello, Mrs Pearce," Andi said, smiling.

Jango Pearce, a plump man with tufts of grey hair on either side of his head, came out to greet them. He was wearing an apron decorated with palm trees and a baseball cap with a huge sunflower sprouting from the top. "What do you think of my new hat?" he asked, turning his head to give them a side view.

"It's certainly bright, Mr Pearce," Andi said carefully.

"That's good! There's no place in Lancashire as sunny as the Banana Beach."

Long John Silver sidled over to the milk jug and tried to dip his beak into it.

"No, you don't," Mrs Pearce scolded, tapping his head.

The parrot hopped away. "Bananas," he grumbled. "More bananas." He gave a sudden shriek that made everyone jump.

"Just listen to that bird!" Mr Pearce chuckled. "He sure knows how to get attention."

"What can I get you?" asked Mrs Pearce.

"Three Banana Spice smoothies, please," Tristan said.

"Three?"

"Natalie's outside with the dogs," he explained.

"You go sit down and I'll bring them right out," Mrs Pearce said, as Mr Pearce disappeared through the beaded curtain to make the smoothies.

Andi and Tristan went outside and sat down. "We must be crazy, sitting outside in November," Andi said, shivering.

"You shouldn't be cold," Natalie said. "You're wearing about twenty layers of clothes."

"Only a jumper, a fleece, and a padded jacket," Andi protested. "What I really need is a couple of blankets and a huge woolly hat to cover my ears."

"You'll get used to the weather here, eventually," Tristan said. "And then you'll wonder what you ever saw in all that Texas sunshine."

Mrs Pearce soon came out carrying a tray of smoothies. There was a rainbow-coloured straw and a yellow paper umbrella in each glass. "Here you go," she said, setting the tray down on the table. "And how are you, Natalie?" she asked.

"I'm fine, thanks, Mrs Pearce."

Mrs Pearce stooped down to stroke the dogs. "You still finding those missing pets?" she asked.

Before they could reply, a deep voice made them all look round. "Hi, Mum."

"Fisher!" Mrs Pearce cried delightedly. "Have you come for dinner?"

"No, just a visit. I'm on my way to make a delivery and then I've got to get back to the RSPCA centre." He was holding a parcel.

Mrs Pearce took his arm. "Now you listen to me, boy. You got to eat right. I know you – having a bite of this here and a bite of that there. Well, it's not good enough. Where are you getting your vitamins? Huh?"

"Mum, I'm—"

"No. You need fattening up. You're too thin and that's bad. You come on in and we'll fix you something good. And you can take some banana brownies home with you."

"Mum, I have to take these calcium pills to Paul Channing. His cat's just had kittens and—"

"We could deliver them for you, if you want," Tristan interrupted, pushing his chair back.

Fisher paused for a moment. "Really?" he asked.

"Definitely. We haven't got much else planned for today."

Andi and Natalie looked at each other, baffled. They had smoothies to finish and Lola to find. They'd never been so busy! What on earth was Tristan thinking?

Chapter Eight

Tristan held out his hand for the package. "It'll save you having to go all the way over there if we deliver it for you," he said persuasively.

"Well, if you're sure . . ." Fisher handed him the parcel. "You'll have to take it to Mr Channing's office, though. It's too big to go through the letterbox at his house. He works at Trantor Insurance in Market Square."

Now Andi knew why Tristan had offered to deliver the pills – he'd hoped they would find out where Mr Channing worked! And he'd got lucky! Giving Natalie a swift kick under the table, she drained her glass and stood up.

"Good thinking, Tristan," Natalie said when they were out of earshot. "Now we'll be able to try out

Dean's plan and take Mr Channing's route home."

"We'd better run," Andi said. "It'll be dark soon." She sped up and Buddy raced along beside her.

"Hang on! Slow down!" Tristan called, running after her.

Andi slowed down to let them catch up, though she was eager to start the search. The light was fading fast now and she hated to think that they might have to wait until tomorrow.

"What a pain!" groaned Tristan as he and Natalie reached her.

"What's up?" Andi asked.

"We passed my mum and dad's estate agency, and my dad was looking out of the window."

"What's wrong with that?" Andi was mystified.

"He gave Tristan a thumbs-up," Natalie chuckled. "I bet he was overjoyed to see you getting some exercise, Tris."

Buddy barked. "I think he's telling us to get a move on," Andi said. "Come on. If we don't hurry, it'll be too dark to see a thing between Market Square and Windrush Drive. Lola could be sitting on the pavement under our feet and we wouldn't notice." She glanced up at the sky and her heart sank: it was charcoal-grey now, with only a narrow band of brightness in the western sky. "It's too late," she sighed. "We'll have to search tomorrow."

They all fell silent, thinking of poor Lola having to spend another night in a strange place.

"Come on," Natalie said. "We can't stand here all night feeling miserable. We've got to deliver these pills."

They ran again, but this time Andi slowed her pace to match Tristan's and Natalie's.

When they reached Market Square, Tristan looked up at the tall office building and made a face. "I bet he works on the top floor."

"There'd better be a lift," Natalie puffed. "I've had more than enough exercise for one day."

"I'll take the tablets in," Andi said, "while you two get your breath back." She handed Buddy's lead to Natalie and sprinted up the steps to the revolving door.

After leaving the parcel with the receptionist, she went outside again to find Tristan and Natalie slumped on the steps as if they'd just finished the London Marathon. "All done," she said. "I suppose we might as well go home."

"What will we be looking for tomorrow, exactly?" Natalie asked.

"A hiding place for a cat," Andi replied. "A garden shed or something, that Lola could have got shut in. Or a tree she might be stuck in. We've got to think about what she might have done if she'd found herself lost outside, and got scared."

"We'll need a map," Tristan suggested. "I don't know the business part of Aldcliffe all that well."

Natalie stood up and smoothed creases from her jeans. "We'll find Lola tomorrow. I'm sure of it."

"I hope you're right," Andi said, crossing her fingers inside the pocket of her jacket, "for Lola's sake."

Tristan and Natalie were waiting for Andi when she arrived in Market Square the next day after school. She'd run home to fetch Buddy.

"Where's Jet, Natalie?" she asked.

"You know what he's like around cats. He'd probably scare Lola away if he spotted her." Natalie patted Buddy. "Not like you, Bud. You know how to behave properly."

"*Most* of the time," Andi laughed. "Though,

actually, he's pretty bad when it comes to cats. But I'll hold his lead tightly so he can't get near Lola – if we find her." She looked round. "Which way, Tristan?"

"Follow me," he said, unfolding his map.

They started off in the business district of Aldcliffe where there were no gardens, and the few trees around were too small and spindly to hide a cat, but they peered hopefully under parked cars as they went by.

After about half a mile, the offices gave way to houses and blocks of flats. They were crammed close together, with narrow strips of garden in between them.

Suddenly, Buddy started straining against his lead. "Do you think he can smell Lola?" Tristan asked excitedly.

They hurried forward, letting Buddy guide them. He sprang over a low wall and into the narrow garden of a block of flats, nearly pulling Andi's arm out of its socket. Tristan and Natalie scrambled after them.

"It looks like he's really on to something," Tristan panted, as Buddy dived into a clump of bushes.

Andi pushed her way after him, wincing as brambles scratched against her face. *Bud had better be on the trail of something worthwhile*, she thought. The bushes were so thick, she couldn't even see Buddy on the end of the lead.

Suddenly the lead went slack and Andi stopped hurriedly before she stepped on her dog by mistake.

"What's he found?" Natalie called. "Is it Lola?"

Andi pushed aside some leaves, holding her breath, and found Buddy rooting excitedly under the lid of a discarded pizza box. Andi's shoulders slumped. "Just an old pizza box." She pulled Buddy back. "Leave it, Bud."

"What a nuisance!" Tristan grumbled when they were back on the pavement.

They crossed and re-crossed the street so they could look on both sides. As they approached Windrush Drive, they walked more slowly. Andi's spirits sank with every step. They'd soon be at Mr Channing's house; if they didn't find any clues to Lola's disappearance in the next few gardens, they could be out of luck. This could turn out to be the first case they wouldn't solve. Andi bit her lip as she remembered how easy finding one pregnant cat had sounded at first.

"What a waste of time," Tristan sighed, echoing her gloomy thoughts. "Trust Dean to come up with a useless idea."

"It might have worked," Natalie said loyally, turning red.

"But it didn't. So what now?"

"I don't know," Andi replied heavily. She couldn't bear to think about giving up – not when Mrs Giacomo was relying on them. And not when poor Lola was out there somewhere, lost and frightened. But what else could they do? They couldn't scour every street in Aldcliffe, hoping to pass by an area that Mr Channing had been through.

Dejectedly, they turned into Windrush Drive and halted outside Mr Channing's house. "That's that, then," Tristan said, sitting on the garden wall. "I'm stumped."

"We can't give up," Natalie said. "We've got to keep looking."

"Jogging!" Andi exclaimed.

Tristan and Natalie stared at her. "You want to go

jogging now?" Tristan asked in astonishment. "Do you ever stop exercising?"

"Not me. Mr Channing. I think he goes jogging. I just remembered. I saw his running shoes and gym bag in the hall when we went to look at the kittens."

"So?"

"So he might have seen Lola when he was jogging. If he has a regular route, we could follow him. Let's come back early tomorrow morning and see where he goes."

"How do you know he goes jogging in the *mornings*?" Tristan asked.

"I don't, but it's worth a try."

Natalie shuddered. "I am *not* getting out of bed early in the morning to go jogging!"

"You'll come, won't you, Tris?" Andi asked.

Tristan frowned. "How early exactly?"

"Half past six?"

"Half past six!" He leapt off the wall. "Nobody gets up at half past six for exercise!"

"Actually, a lot of people do. Say you'll come. I don't want to follow him on my own."

"Half past six," Tristan groaned, "is the middle of the night."

"Please, Tris. It'll be worth it if it leads us to Lola. You said yourself Mrs Giacomo is depending on us."

He frowned, then nodded reluctantly. "Okay. But don't anyone tell my dad what I'm up to. I don't want him thinking I've turned into a fitness freak."

It was bitterly cold the next morning when Andi slipped out of the house. She ran extra fast to keep warm and by twenty past six she was turning into Windrush Drive. The houses were dark and the streetlights were still on, but above the mountains the sky was lightening.

Tristan arrived soon after. "You made it then," Andi said, grinning. He looked half-asleep.

"Don't," he groaned. "It's too early for conversation."

They sat on a garden wall and waited for Mr Channing to come out of his house. There was no sign of life in the Channings' house and Andi began to wonder if she'd got it wrong. Maybe Mr Channing wasn't a morning jogger after all.

It was nearly seven o'clock when the landing light suddenly went on in his house. "This could be it," Andi whispered.

The front door opened. "There he is!" Andi leapt back behind some branches that overhung the pavement. She pulled Tristan after her.

As they'd hoped, Mr Channing came out of the house dressed in running gear. He jogged straight down his driveway and then along the pavement away from them.

"Come on." Andi began to run after him.

"Can't I just wait for you here?" Tristan muttered.

"No! Come on!"

Tristan sprinted to catch up with her. "I hope he doesn't go far," he panted.

Mr Channing reached the end of the road and turned right. Andi and Tristan followed at a safe distance. As they passed Tangletree House, Andi looked down at the pavement. She was glad Tristan was with her, though he was puffing so hard she couldn't imagine him being much help if a ghost suddenly materialized.

They rounded the corner just in time to see Mr Channing turning right again. "It looks as though he's only going round the block," Andi said, disappointed. They'd already searched this area thoroughly.

"Thank goodness," Tristan puffed. "I can't keep going much longer."

As they reached the next corner, they stopped dead in dismay. Mr Channing was waiting for them, looking very upset. "You again!" he said fiercely. "Are you following me?"

Andi and Tristan stopped, shocked. "N-No," Andi stuttered. "We're searching for Mrs Giacomo's cat, that's all."

"At *this* time of day?"

"At *any* time of day," Tristan puffed, standing his ground. "Lola's pregnant. We've got to find her quickly."

"Pregnant?" Mr Channing's jaw dropped. "I didn't know! Helen never mentioned that."

"That's why we're searching so hard," Andi told him.

Mr Channing nodded. "Yes, yes. I see. I suppose this does change things." He smiled half-heartedly.

"What does it change?" Tristan demanded.

"Oh, no, nothing. I just understand the urgency now," replied Mr Channing nervously. "Well, I hope you find her soon." He turned quickly and jogged away.

"Phew," Andi said when he was out of earshot. "That was scary." She grinned at Tristan. "You were great, Tris. I'm glad you were here."

"Thanks." He glanced at his watch. "It looks as though you were right about him only jogging round the block. If he went any further, he'd be late for work."

"So if he did see Lola when he was jogging, it must have been around here. Perhaps we missed something when we were looking before."

"Let's come back after school and have another look," Tristan suggested.

"OK."

"That's if my legs haven't fallen off," Tristan added, sinking down on a garden wall. "I don't suppose you'd give me a piggyback home, would you?"

Andi laughed. "No chance!"

The Pet Finders hurried down to Windrush Drive after school. But, even though they'd got out of school as quickly as they could, and Andi had persuaded Tristan and Natalie to jog most of the way to her house to grab Buddy, an early autumn dusk was already settling over the rooftops. The mountains on the horizon seemed to have sucked the light out of the sky, leaving only a pale creamy strip at the edge of dark grey clouds. It was much darker than Andi would have liked for exploring near a house with so many haunting legends surrounding it.

"Do you think we'll find anything?" Natalie asked as they stopped on the corner. "We were pretty thorough before."

Andi shrugged. "We've got to do something and this is the only lead we've got."

They set off along the pavement. Tangletree House lay ahead of them, crouching beside the building site like a sleeping giant. A cold shiver ran down Andi's spine. The boarded-up windows made her nervous. She couldn't help wondering if someone – or something – was hidden behind them, watching their every move through the narrow gaps between the wall planks.

As they passed the building site beside the house, they heard a muffled cry.

"What was that?" Natalie gasped, clutching Andi's arm.

The hairs on the back of Andi's neck prickled once again. "I don't know."

They stood still, listening hard over the thudding of their hearts.

"Help!" called a panic-stricken voice. "Help us!"

"Well, that didn't sound like a ghost," said Tristan.

The Pet Finders ran to the chain-link fence in front of the house and peered through. There was nothing to see except the house, the stretch of cleared, muddy ground in front of it where new pipes were being laid, and the line of tangled shrubs and trees still growing beside it. Through the shrubs, they could just make out the main building site with its yawning holes, half-built walls and bulldozers.

"Who's there?" Tristan called.

"Hello? Anyone? Help!" The voice was coming from beyond the shrubs.

"Don't answer, Tris," Natalie hissed.

"Uh, you don't believe in ghosts," Andi reminded her.

"D-d-didn't," Natalie corrected through chattering teeth. "But you saw the way the dogs behaved last time we were here. And all those people at school believe they've seen or heard something, too. Perhaps I was wrong."

"But it doesn't *sound* like a ghost," Tristan insisted, moving along the pavement in the direction of the voice.

The voice came again. "Please help! We've fallen in a hole!"

"Well, that's either the most cunning ghost I've ever heard of, or some kids have got trapped," said Tristan. He dumped his rucksack on the ground and pushed up his sleeves. "Come on, we'll have to get them out."

"What if the ghost comes while we're in there?" Natalie quavered. "Maybe they fell into the hole when they were running away from it!"

Andi tried not to listen. She wanted to run away too.

"We can't leave them," Tristan said. He tried to climb up the fence, but the holes in the mesh were too small for his trainers.

"We're not allowed in there," Andi warned him. "You heard what Miss Ashworthy and Mr Dixon said."

"But it's an emergency," Tristan said. "The teachers only meant nobody should go inside to mess around."

"It's a shame those kids in there didn't listen then," Natalie said sharply. Sighing, she pulled out her mobile phone. "I'll call the police and they'll come and pull them out."

"No! They'll get into trouble," Tristan pointed out.

"Tris is right," Andi agreed. "We ought to help them ourselves. But we'll have to be careful." She glanced across at Tangletree House, wishing she was anywhere but there.

They searched along the fence for a way in. "Over here," Tristan called, finding a place where the wire had come away from its post. "This must be where they got in."

With trembling hands, Natalie bent the mesh back to make the gap as wide as possible. She looked down at her jeans which were streaked with rust, and shrugged. "They just look old-old now, not designer-old."

Andi squeezed Natalie's arm. She could tell her friend was genuinely scared to go on to the site. "We'll be all right in there," she said, trying to reassure herself as much as Natalie. She handed Buddy's lead to Tristan and then, taking a deep breath, crawled through the gap.

Standing up, Andi looked round. Long dark holes were yawning out of the ground just a few metres away. Beyond them stood half-built brick walls. To her left, half hidden behind the tangle of shrubs, Tangletree House loomed over them.

Buddy began to whine. "It's OK, Bud," Andi told him. "You can come, too." She reached through the hole and took his lead from Tristan. He scampered through the gap, then jumped up at her, clearly relieved that they were together again.

Natalie and Tristan crawled through. Natalie frowned at the churned-up earth in front of them. "Do we really have to tramp through this?"

"Looks like it," Tristan said, sounding as if he was making a huge effort to stay cheerful.

Andi began to feel a bit better. There were three of them, after all, and they had Buddy with them. "Come on," she said. "We'd better find those kids quickly if we're not supposed to be here." She raised her voice. "Where are you?" she called.

"Over here!"

"Keep yelling so we know which direction to take."

They moved forward, following the sound of a

116

boy's voice and trying to skirt round the worst of the mud. The ground had been so badly turned over by bulldozers and dumper trucks that their trainers were soon thickly caked and weighed about twenty times more than usual.

"This is horrible!" Natalie said.

"That's building sites for you," Tristan pointed out.

"I don't just mean the mud. I mean everything." She meant the ghost that was supposed to haunt Tangletree House.

Andi squelched along, keeping her gaze fixed on the ground. She was determined not to look at the old house. "There's no such thing as ghosts," she muttered under her breath. "There's no such thing as ghosts." If only she could convince herself that it was true . . .

Chapter Nine

"Where are you?" the boy called. He sounded much closer now. "Hurry up!"

"We're almost there!" Tristan called back. "The hole must be really deep," he added in a low voice. "I can't see them at all. I hope we can get them out."

"Me too," Andi agreed grimly.

Struggling to keep their footing in the slippery mud, the Pet Finders skirted round a huge stack of bricks. Passing two mud-spattered bulldozers, they found themselves on the edge of a trench that was longer and deeper than all the others.

Andi held Buddy's lead tightly, afraid that he might fall in.

"At least they had a soft landing, with all this mud," Tristan muttered.

"True," Andi agreed.

Suddenly, her foot slipped. For a moment, she teetered on the very edge of the trench, flapping her arms in a desperate attempt to keep her balance. Below her, she could see three mud-plastered figures, one sitting and two standing. They were gazing up at her, open-mouthed with dismay.

"Andi!" Tristan yelled. He grabbed her around the waist and jerked her back from the edge.

Andi let out a long, shuddering breath. "Thanks, Tris," she gasped. "That was close."

"Are you all right?" Natalie asked, concerned.

Andi nodded. She was shaken, but she wasn't hurt. And at least they'd found the kids.

The hole was about three metres deep. "Can you get us out?" called one of the boys. He was tall and broad-shouldered and he wore a muddy, hooded top. "Kenny and I are OK, but Brad's hurt his ankle." He pointed to a thin boy with spiky hair who was sitting in the mud, clutching his ankle.

"We're going to need a rope," said Tristan.

"Maybe there'll be one under here," Andi suggested, spotting a lumpy tarpaulin nearby. She heaved up the edge to discover an untidy heap of buckets, shovels, pick-axes, bags of cement, boxes of nails and rolls of roofing felt. Andi searched through the heap, then gave a triumphant shout. "Got one!" Miraculously, there was a rope coiled neatly inside one of the buckets. It looked thick enough to hold her weight and she felt a sudden surge of reassurance.

Dragging the rope out from under the tarpaulin, Andi tied one end round the trunk of a nearby tree and lowered the other end into the hole. "Hold on," she called down to the boys. "I'll come down and give you a hand."

"Be careful, Andi," Tristan warned.

"I'll be fine," Andi assured him, trying to ignore the lump in her throat. It suddenly looked a very long way down to the bottom of the hole. She handed Buddy's lead to Natalie. "Stay, Bud," she commanded.

Buddy gazed up at her miserably. He hated being left behind.

"It's all right, boy. I'll be quick," Andi promised. She wiped her muddy hands on her sweatshirt before grabbing hold of the rope. Taking a deep breath, she swung herself over the edge of the pit.

Natalie and Tristan watched her anxiously.

"I thought we were supposed to be saving pets, not people," Andi called up to them, trying to ease the tension. Natalie smiled weakly and Tristan managed a half-hearted laugh.

Andi knew she had reached the bottom of the rope when she sank up to her ankles in mud. "Yuck!" she groaned.

Two of the boys waded across to her. "That was quite a climb," one of them said, impressed. "I'm Carl."

"I'm Andi. Can you climb up there?" she asked.

"I should think so. Kenny, hold the rope tight for me." Carl began to haul himself up the rope, grunting and puffing with the effort.

Andi crouched beside Brad. His ankle was bruised and swollen. "That looks pretty bad," she said sympathetically.

"Yeah. I won't be able to climb that rope."

"The others will have to pull you up." Andi glanced round. Carl had reached the top of the rope and was standing on the edge of the pit with Tristan and Natalie. "Come on, Kenny," he called. "Get a move on."

Kenny was dangling a little way off the ground. "Can you hold the rope still for me?" he panted, looking at Andi. "I can't get a grip with it swinging around like this."

Andi seized the end of the rope and held it taut.

"Thanks." Kenny began to climb. Slowly, slowly he inched his way up, red-faced with effort, his arms shaking with weight and tension. When he was almost at the top, he started slipping down again. "Help!" he yelled.

Tristan let go of the rope and reached down to him. "Grab my hand. I'll pull you up."

"I can't," Kenny wailed, sliding down even further.

Tristan and Carl knelt in the mud and leant over as far as they could. "Come on!" Tristan called. "You can do it."

Kenny looked up at him despairingly, then made a lunge for his hand. Tristan caught him by the wrist, Carl caught his other hand, and together they hauled him up out of sight from Andi and Brad at the bottom of the hole.

"I'm going to tie the rope around Brad," Andi called. "You'll have to pull him up, then drop the rope down to me again so I can climb out." She hauled Brad to his feet, then helped him hobble to the side of the pit.

"OK!" she called. "He's ready."

Natalie held Buddy's lead while Tristan, Kenny, and Carl seized the rope. They began to pull.

Brad was lifted off his feet. He dangled for a moment, turning slowly like a broken puppet, then began to rise jerkily into the air.

In a few long moments, he'd reached the top. He sank down in the mud, gasping and clutching his injured ankle. Tristan then untied the rope and dropped it down to Andi.

"Thanks," she said. She wiped her hands on her jeans to remove the worst of the mud, then swung herself easily up the rope.

Buddy started barking madly as she emerged from the hole. The moment she landed, he leapt up at her, making her jeans muddier than ever.

"It's OK, Bud," Andi said. "I'm back now, though I don't know how I'm going to explain all this mud to Mum . . ." She shrugged. "Oh well, at least we've got our new washing machine."

"That was amazing, Andi," said Tristan, as they

coiled the rope and put it back under the tarpaulin. "Where did you learn to climb like that?"

Andi shrugged. "Back in Texas. I always loved PE lessons."

"It shows," Tristan told her. "I've never seen anyone climb like that. Except monkeys, of course," he added with a grin.

Andi aimed a playful slap at him, but he dodged.

"What were you doing on the building site?" Natalie asked the boys.

Carl looked down at his feet. "Ghost-hunting."

"We didn't believe there was a ghost," Kenny added. "Not really." His eyes stretched wide with fear. "Until we heard it."

"It was wailing," Carl said shakily. "So we ran for it. That was how we fell down that hole."

"I knew it," Natalie muttered to Andi. "Let's get out of here."

Kenny and Carl supported Brad as they headed for the gap in the fence. Andi, Tristan, and Natalie followed with Buddy.

"How's Brad going to get through the hole in the fence?" Natalie asked. "He can't put any weight on that ankle."

"We'll have to go out by the main gate," said Carl. "The one right in front of the house." He didn't need to say what was on everyone's mind: that this would mean going much closer to the haunted ruin.

Natalie leant close to Andi. "Buddy will protect us if we see anything, won't he?" she whispered.

"We won't see anything," Andi replied, hoping that she was right.

They reached the tangle of shrubs that grew beside Tangletree House. "We'll have to go between these bushes and the house wall," Tristan said. "It's the only way to reach the main gate."

Fearfully, Andi looked up at the house; it seemed bigger and spookier than ever, and it was all too easy to imagine a whole army of ghosts inside, just waiting for the right moment to drift through the walls and surround them.

They set off along the narrow path, moving as quietly as they could. Low branches snatched at their clothes with thorny fingers, and Andi's hair stood on end every time something brushed against her face.

"Oh, this is hopeless!" Natalie groaned, stopping

to untangle her sleeve from a bramble. "We'll never get out of here at this rate . . ."

Just then, her words were drowned out by a hideous, shrieking, ghostly wail.

Chapter Ten

"It's the ghost!" Carl yelled.

"Let's get out of here!" Kenny wailed. He and Carl let go of Brad and sprinted off round the front of the house.

Brad dropped to the ground with a gasp of pain. "My ankle!"

Andi's heart leapt into her throat and stayed there. Fighting back the fear that told her to get out of there immediately, she ran over and seized Brad's arm. "Help me get him up, Nat!" she panted. "We can't leave him here."

Natalie grabbed Brad's other arm and they hauled him to his feet, then half-carried, half-dragged him along the path. Twigs and thorns snagged painfully in Andi's hair as she stumbled along. What if the ghost appeared now? They'd never outrun it with Brad slowing them down.

They reached the corner of the house. The gate leading to the street stood open about thirty metres away. There was no sign of Carl or Kenny.

Andi and Natalie headed for the gate, with Buddy scampering beside them. "Nearly there," Andi gasped. She looked back, expecting to see Tristan hard on their heels. But he was standing beside a veranda that ran along the front of the haunted house, staring at a boarded-up window.

"Tristan!" Andi yelled. "Come on! We've got to go!"

He didn't move.

"Tristan!" she cried again.

"He must have seen the ghost!" Natalie gasped hoarsely. "He's too scared to move. We'll have to go back for him."

They sat Brad down on a tree stump and darted back.

"Wait!" he called after them. "Don't leave me!"

"We've got to help Tristan!" Natalie puffed. "We'll come back for you in a minute."

Andi reached Tristan first. She grabbed his

arm and tried to pull him away. "Tristan! You've got to come."

"No, wait." He shook her off. "Look at the window."

Andi looked at it fearfully, expecting to see a pair of evil eyes peering through a crack, but there was nothing to see except planks nailed across the gap where glass used to be. "What?" she asked.

"That plank's been moved." Sure enough, one of the planks had slid down a little, leaving a narrow opening.

"So?" Andi was feeling a little less scared now – it was hard to stay spooked when Tristan was pointing out gaps in planks.

Natalie reached them. "Come on, Tristan," she quavered.

"But why would a ghost move a plank? Ghosts can walk through walls." Tristan looked at Andi and Natalie, his eyes thoughtful. "That plank was definitely fixed across the window when I came past here on Wednesday morning. I was helping Dean with his paper round and we were joking about the number of papers he'd have to deliver when all this building work's finished. We counted the windows to see if we could work out how many flats there'll be, and there was no gap then."

"How can you be so sure?" Natalie pressed.

"I just am. I remember things like that. You know, like the Sun-Fruit number off that lorry."

Suddenly Buddy gave a loud whine and jerked on his lead.

The Pet Finders nearly jumped out of their skins. Andi groaned, getting ready to run as if all the football try-outs in the world depended on it.

"No, wait!" Tristan cried. "Look, Buddy's pulling towards the house, not away from it. He wants to go *inside!*"

It was true: Buddy was straining towards the house. And he didn't seem at all frightened. His ears were pricked up and his tail was wagging.

"I want a closer look at that plank," Tristan continued. He swallowed hard. "Will you come with me?"

Andi's stomach lurched, but she could see that Tristan wasn't going anywhere until he'd investigated properly, and they couldn't leave him on his own. "OK," she agreed.

"What are you doing?" Brad called. "Don't leave me!"

"We won't be long," Andi promised.

They walked up the steps on to the veranda, then crept along it, carefully avoiding the rotten planks. When they were almost at the window, the eerie wail sang out, freezing them in their tracks.

But if Andi was being honest with herself, Buddy still didn't look the least bit scared: if anything, he seemed excited.

As the unearthly sound died away, Tristan spoke in a low voice: "Come on. We still need to look at that window."

"Don't, Tristan," Natalie quavered. "Let's get out of here."

"No, wait," Andi urged. "If Tristan's on to something, we should investigate."

"We're the *Pet* Finders, remember?" Natalie said. "That means we should be investigating pets, right? Not ghosts."

"Come on," Tristan said. "It'll be all right."

They tiptoed forward again. In a few steps, they reached the window and gathered round it, trembling.

"There!" Tristan hissed. "What's that you were saying, Nat?" A small clump of blue-grey hairs was clinging to the edge of the window frame. "I think we might have found a missing pet after all!"

"Lola," they all whispered together.

"This must be where Mr Channing saw her. He jogged right past here, even if it *is* just around his own block." Andi licked her dry lips. "We'll have to go in and look for her."

"What about the ghost?" Natalie gasped.

"There is no ghost," Andi said. She suddenly realized that there had been something rather familiar about the wailing that had spooked them so much. "I think all that yowling was Lola, trying to get out."

"But Larissa's cousin – or friend – or whoever – *saw* something."

"Maybe he imagined it. Maybe he heard Lola and was frightened by a shadow or something."

"And what if he didn't imagine it?" Natalie persisted. "What if there *is* a ghost inside? The legends about this place are much older than Lola's disappearance."

Andi rubbed her hands together, trying to stop

them from trembling. She couldn't tell Natalie absolutely that there weren't any ghosts inside the house, however logical she made it sound. "There's only one way to find out."

They tiptoed back along the veranda to the front door.

"What are you doing *now?*" Brad called, as Tristan opened the door a crack.

"We'll be as quick as we can!" Tristan promised. He pressed his eye to the crack. "I can't see anything."

"At least leave me your dog for protection!" Brad begged. "I don't want to be by myself!"

The Pet Finders looked at each other. "I suppose we could leave Buddy out here," Andi said. "It'll keep him from trying to chase Lola when we find her."

"*If* we find her," Natalie said.

Andi led the little dog over to Brad. "Stay, Bud," she said, patting him.

"Thanks." Brad looked a little happier as he hugged Buddy. "I'll keep an eye on him. Don't worry."

Andi ran back to the others. "Let's go."

Natalie looked back at her with huge, anxious eyes. "Look, do you really think this is a good idea? We're going to get into a lot more trouble for going inside the house than we are for just being in the garden."

Tristan rolled his eyes. "How can we call ourselves Pet Finders if we don't even try looking?" he asked impatiently. He put his shoulder against the door and braced himself to give it a shove.

Wham! The door flew open and crashed back against the inside wall, sending Tristan staggering into the hallway with arms flailing. Andi bit her lip to stop a nervous giggle from bursting out.

Tristan dusted his hands off, annoyed. "Well, are you coming in?" he demanded.

Andi glanced at Natalie and nodded. Taking a deep breath, they stepped through the old doorframe and followed Tristan into the house.

As soon as they shuffled through the door, it swung shut behind them, plunging them into gloom. The only light came from the narrow gaps between the planks that were covering the window, and for a moment Andi couldn't see a thing. The lump in her throat was back, and she was convinced that someone – some*thing* – was about to grab her. Then her eyes grew accustomed to the dimness and she saw that they were in an enormous entrance hall. Muddy boot trails led across the floor to a broad flight of stairs with ornate wooden banisters. Somehow it didn't seem quite as scary knowing that the builders had been in here already.

"Which way?" Natalie breathed.

Andi looked round uncertainly. The old house was massive – it would take them forever to search every room.

Suddenly the shrill wail sounded again, louder than ever.

Even though she told herself over and over again that the unearthly sound *was* Lola, Andi's heart flipped over and her hands became clammy. She wished that she'd brought Buddy inside after all. It would have been reassuring to feel his warmth against her leg. But there was no time to go back and get him: Lola needed to be rescued, and fast.

"That came from upstairs," she said, sounding much braver than she felt. She led the way over to the stairs and started to climb. Each step creaked under their feet, as if they were walking through the set of an old horror movie. Andi resisted the urge to giggle out loud.

At the top of the stairs, a long landing stretched away in both directions. Which way now?

"Lola!" Andi called. "Where are you, girl?" Her voice echoed along the corridor.

There was an answering wail. Now that they could hear it clearly, it was definitely a cat in distress.

"Down there!" Natalie said, sounding much less frightened now.

They sped along the landing, following Lola's cry. Racing through a half-open door, they found themselves in a bathroom. A new white bath and shining silver taps gleamed in the twilight: the builders had evidently only just finished work in there.

"Lola!" Andi called again. "Where are you, girl?"

A dismal howl came from under a wooden panel that ran alongside the bath. Andi flung herself down beside it and pressed her eye to a crack. A pair of glittering eyes looked back at her, like green flames in the darkness. Andi lurched back. "It's those eyes!" she croaked.

"What? What is it?" Natalie demanded, backing away from the bath.

Cautiously, Andi peered through the crack again. The eyes were still there and the wail sounded again. "They're Lola's eyes!" she exclaimed.

As Lola's wail died away, she heard a chorus of tiny yelps.

"So you can see her?" Tristan asked.

"Yes! And I think she's had her kittens!"

Chapter Eleven

"Help me get this panel off," Andi said. She tried to squeeze her fingers into the gap between the wooden panel and the wall, but it was too narrow.

"Try lifting it from the bottom," Tristan suggested, crouching beside her. Natalie knelt at the far end and they pulled together, but the panel was too firmly fixed.

"The builders must have screwed it in place," Andi groaned.

They searched frantically for a screwdriver but the workers hadn't left any tools behind.

"Poor Lola," Andi said desperately. "She must have been cooped up in there for days. We've got to get her out fast."

But the wooden panel stayed put.

"Give me your phone, Natalie!" Tristan said suddenly.

"Who are you ringing?" Andi asked.

"The fire brigade. And then I'll call Fisher so he can come and check Lola and her kittens."

Andi crouched beside the bath. "It's OK, girl," she told the frightened cat. "We're going to get you out of there." She couldn't see or hear Lola any more, but she could hear the occasional faint meow from the kittens. "Mrs Giacomo's going to be so happy we've found you."

The fire brigade arrived in a fire engine with its siren blaring and blue lights flashing. Tristan went to meet them, and Andi listened to Lola's rescuers pounding up the stairs.

"She's under the bath," Andi said when the men appeared in the doorway, looking reassuring in their broad-shouldered maroon jackets. "But we can't get the panel off."

"Stand back," said one of them, heaving a tool box into the tiny room.

Andi and Natalie scrambled up and squeezed into the far corner. Andi had pins and needles from crouching down for so long and she shook each foot in turn as the firemen set about removing the panel.

They heard more footsteps on the landing, then a stocky, dark-haired man appeared. "What's going on?" he demanded.

"A cat's trapped under this bath," Tristan explained.

"Trapped? It can't be. My workmen put that bath in days ago. There's no way a cat could have got underneath there since then. They always do a good job."

"She must have slipped under while they were fitting it," Andi said. "Maybe when they stopped for a break. And then they fixed the panel in place and she was trapped."

The builder pushed back his baseball hat and scratched his head. "And she's been in there all this time? Poor thing. I suppose we'd never have heard her during the day – this is a pretty noisy place when everyone's working."

There was a loud cracking sound as one of the firemen used a screwdriver to pry at the wooden panel, and the builder frowned. "Hey, be careful!

This is a top-of-the-range bathroom suite!"

Andi opened her mouth to protest that Lola and her kittens were much more important than any bathroom unit, but she caught Natalie giving her a warning glance and quickly stopped. There was another creak that made the builder wince, and then a deafening pop when the wood was finally snapped from the wall. The two firemen stepped away carrying the panel between them, and there was Lola, crouched protectively in front of three tiny, fluffy kittens. Her fur was covered in dust and grime, and she was blinking hard in the sudden burst of light, but she was obviously determined to stay with her little family.

"Oh, Lola!" Andi whispered. "I can't believe we've found you!"

"Well I'm blowed!" said the foreman. "The men aren't going to believe me when I tell them about this."

Tristan gently lifted Lola up. He turned on the bath tap and let cold water run into his hand. Lola lapped thirstily, then snuggled down in his arms as if she knew he'd come to rescue her.

The kittens came tottering towards the light,

their eyes tight shut and their tiny tails stuck straight up in the air. "Oh, they're so sweet!" Natalie exclaimed. She scooped one up and held it against her chest.

Andi picked up the last two kittens. They were soft and warm, and began to purr in tiny rumbling voices as she cradled them.

The firemen crowded round to stroke the cats, their hands giant and clumsy in their protective gloves. "Lucky you kids found them," said the one who had carried the tools.

Suddenly they heard Fisher's voice. "Hello? Is anyone here?"

"In here!" Tristan called back.

Fisher came into the bathroom. "You've found your missing Russian Blue, then," he said, beaming at them. "Good work! Let me see her." He pulled out his stethoscope and listened to Lola's chest. Then he checked her ears and eyes. "How long do you think she's been shut in?"

"Mrs Giacomo said she disappeared nearly a week ago," Tristan replied.

Fisher smiled. "You'd never know it. She's perfectly fit." He scratched Lola's ears and she

rubbed her head against his hand. "I should think she's been catching mice to keep her strength up." He checked the kittens one by one. "And there's nothing wrong with these beauties either. You three did a great job of tracking them down!"

"Thanks!" said Andi. She grinned at Natalie and Tristan.

"We'd better go," Natalie said. "We don't want to keep Mrs Giacomo waiting."

They carried Lola and her kittens downstairs. As they came outside, they saw a policeman speaking to Carl, Kenny, and Brad. "All the schools in the area have warned children to keep away from this building site," he said sternly. "So what on earth were you doing in here?"

The three boys hung their heads. "We were only wandering around," Carl muttered.

"Hey, Gerry," one of the firemen called to the policeman.

The policeman glanced around. "Hi, Tim. I saw your engine and came to see if I could help. Then I spotted these three. Two of them had come back to look for their friend, who hurt his ankle falling into a pit." He gave an exaggerated sigh. "Honestly, can't kids see the danger in playing on building sites?"

Buddy spotted Andi and jumped up, barking a greeting. "Do you think you can hold all three kittens, Natalie?" Andi asked. "I think Buddy's feeling a bit jealous."

"You bet," Natalie said. Her voice had gone all dreamy, like it had when she'd been looking at Snowdrop's kittens.

The policeman caught sight of the Pet Finders. "Good grief, more kids! Now you listen to me—"

"They only came to help us!" Carl told him quickly. "They heard us yelling."

"And they've saved the lives of a cat and her kittens," Fisher added.

The policeman's eyebrows shot up. "Is that right? They're local heroes for trespassing?" He shook his head. "It sounds a bit cockeyed to me." He turned back to Carl, Kenny, and Brad. "I'll be speaking to your head teacher about finding you three here. And if I ever catch you on a building site again—"

"You won't," Brad said quickly, rubbing his swollen ankle.

"Definitely not," Kenny and Carl promised.

"I'm glad to hear it." The policeman headed for his car.

"That ankle looks as though it needs some attention," Fisher said. "Would you boys like a lift home?"

"Yes, please," Brad replied. Kenny and Carl helped him limp over to the gate.

"How far are you going with these cats?" one of the firemen asked.

"Just round the corner," Tristan said. "Scayne Place."

"Do you want a ride in a fire engine?"

The Pet Finders looked at each other, each clearly thinking the same thing.

"YES!" Andi exclaimed.

The fire engine drew up outside Mrs Giacomo's house with a hiss of brakes.

"Thanks for the ride!" Andi said as she leapt down from the cab. Buddy jumped down after her.

Natalie and Tristan climbed down, and the firemen passed Lola and her kittens to them.

"See you!" the men called as they drove away.

"Bye! Thanks for everything!"

As the Pet Finders hurried up the path, they saw Mr Channing standing on the doorstep talking to Mrs Giacomo. He looked agitated. "I know I should have told you before, Helen, but—"

"Yes, you should have!" Mrs Giacomo interrupted angrily. "Lola and her kittens could be—" Her gaze fell on the Pet Finders. "Lola!" she cried. She ran past Mr Channing and swept Lola out of Tristan's arms. "Oh, thank you! Thank you!" She hugged her cat tightly.

"Please don't say anything to the show authorities," Mr Channing pleaded. "It was stupid of me to keep quiet about seeing Princess Anastasia, but I thought it would give one of my cats a chance to win first prize for once. And you've got her back now, so no harm's done."

"I don't want to talk about this now," Mrs Giacomo snapped. "Please go away, Paul." She turned her back on him and beamed at the Pet Finders. "Come in, come in!"

"We're a bit muddy," Natalie said doubtfully.

"Oh, don't worry about that."

"Helen, please—" Mr Channing called as the

Pet Finders followed Mrs Giacomo inside. He tried to follow but she shut the door firmly.

"Lola's had her kittens!" Andi said. "Look."

Mrs Giacomo gave a gasp of delight and spun round to see them. "They're gorgeous," she cooed. "Absolutely beautiful." She sat down with Lola, and Natalie placed the kittens in her lap. "I bet you're wondering why Paul Channing was here," she said, stroking each of the kittens in turn. "Apparently, he saw Lola going into Tangletree House last week. He didn't tell me before because he wanted his cat, Beauty, to win next week's show."

"So why did he come today?" Natalie asked.

"He heard that Lola was pregnant. He felt bad about her condition and he knew she couldn't enter the show with young kittens to care for, anyway." She shook her head, clearly still angry. "I thought we were friends! I should have listened to you children."

"Will you report him?" Andi asked.

"I don't know. I'll have to think about that." Mrs Giacomo laughed. "But I definitely won't be sharing my coffee with him any more at cat shows!"

"We still don't know how Lola got out of your

house," Tristan said. "I think it *must* have been that screen door. Do you mind if we have another look at it?"

"Help yourselves," Mrs Giacomo said.

They went into the kitchen. Andi opened the back door, revealing the familiar screen door. They all stared at it for a few moments, but didn't notice anything peculiar. Then Tristan crouched down and put his hand on the bottom of the door.

"Look at this!" Tristan tilted the door. "The bottom hinge is broken. All you have to do is push a bit and this gap opens up." The space between the door frame and screen was certainly big enough for even a large cat to fit through.

They hurried back to the living room to tell Mrs Giacomo.

"Thank goodness you spotted that," she said. "There's no way I would have noticed it and Lola or Deena might have got out again." She smiled round at them. "I might need one of you to move in here, to keep an eye on us!" She laughed, then became more serious. "Perhaps one of you would like a kitten when they're old enough to leave Lola?"

Andi's heart skipped a beat. The kittens were so

sweet! It would be the best thing ever to have one of her own. Then she glanced down at Buddy who was lying with his head on her feet. Maybe the *second*-best thing ever. Nothing could beat having Buddy around. And it had been hard work looking after Apple as well as Buddy, so Andi knew she only had time for one pet. "Not me, thanks," she said. "I've got Buddy."

"And Jet sometimes chases cats," Natalie said wistfully, "so it wouldn't be fair to the kitten."

They turned to look at Tristan. "How about you, Tris?" Andi prompted. "You haven't got a pet."

He looked down at the kittens. "They're great," he agreed. "But I still think Lucy might come home one day. It would be terrible if she turned up and found a new cat had taken her place."

Andi's heart sank with a thud. "Lucy's been gone a long time," she reminded him gently.

"I know, but . . ." He broke off and forced a smile. "No, thanks, Mrs Giacomo."

"Well, you can still come and see Lola whenever you like," she told them.

After some cocoa, they finally said their goodbyes and headed for home. Andi was very worried about how unhappy Tristan seemed. She wished they could find Lucy for him, but she'd been missing for months. There couldn't possibly be a trail to follow after so long.

"Cheer up, Tris," said Natalie. "The Pet Finders have done it again!"

"It was a great result," Andi agreed. "We started out looking for one lost cat and ended up finding four!"

Tristan nodded. "You're right. There's no point being moody." He grinned. "I wonder what animal we'll be searching for next."

"You never know, we might have to go into *people*-finding as well," Andi joked. "We found Apple's owner and we found Carl, Kenny and Brad."

"I don't mind finding people," Natalie said firmly, hoisting her rucksack on to her shoulder. "Just as long as we don't have to find any ghosts!"

book 4

THE PET FINDERS CLUB

Rescuing Raisin

Do you love animals?

Has your pet ever gone missing?

Well meet Andi, Tristan and Natalie — The Pet Finders Club. Animals don't stay lost for long with them hot on the trail!

The Pet Finders are at their wits' end when a dalmatian disappears without a trace. It seems he was last seen at the train station. Their only hope is that he didn't get on a train... or he could be anywhere by now!